DAD BOD ORC

DAD BOD MONSTER EDITION

TANA STONE

BROADMOOR BOOKS

CHAPTER
ONE

Roc

I rubbed a hand over the bunched muscles in my neck as I pushed back from the desk, my chair rolling across the black, hardwood floors and slowing to a stop before the wheels bumped into the glass wall. I didn't need to crane my sore neck to know that the sun had set long ago. I didn't need to twist around to know that the lights from Los Angeles were flickering behind me. I didn't need to peer out the glass wall of my home office to realize that another day had come and gone without me leaving my enclave high up Mulholland Drive. But I did.

With a groan and a loud exhale, I stood and braced my hands on the glass. The view never got old, even if I didn't enjoy venturing into the city that provided it.

"City of Angels," I said, with a rumbling laugh. As beautiful as the city lights might be, I knew enough of the dark side to shake my head. There were few angels in LA.

Scraping a hand through the dark, shaggy hair that fell to my shoulders, I padded on bare feet from my office to the kitchen. "But there's no shortage of monsters."

This made me chuckle again, since I was one of the inhuman creatures who'd integrated with society and become more human than monster. Sometimes I wondered if I'd assimilated too well and lost too many of my orc ways, especially since I wasn't a pureblood.

I caught a glimpse of my olive-green skin in the reflection of the glass oven door as I headed for the refrigerator. Nope, I still looked like a three-quarter orc, and no amount of stylish, black clothing, or expensive cologne, would change that.

I yanked open the stainless-steel fridge door and grabbed a green juice from the top shelf. At least I didn't crave blood like the vamps. Orcs—especially ones mixed with humans, like me—had been accepted better than most monsters. It helped that we were known for impressive physical strength, which meant we were in high demand in construction work and in the military.

My top lip curled, catching for a moment on one of the small tusks that poked up from my bottom lip. The thought of joining one of the orc construction teams had never appealed to me, but it wasn't because I wasn't as strong as the purebloods. Well, maybe I wasn't, but my less-burly build meant I was quicker and had faster reflexes, both traits that came in handy in my line of work.

My office phone trilled as I twisted off the cap from the juice bottle and took a glug. I checked my watch. Who was calling so late?

I ignored it as I swept my hair up into a man bun and started for my bedroom, unbuttoning my shirt as I went. The office line stopped ringing, but I barely had a chance to enjoy the silence before the phone in my pocket started to vibrate.

"Orc's blood," I cursed, as I retrieved my phone and left my shirt hanging open. I didn't check the number before answering it. Only clients had my cell number, so if someone was calling, it was important. "Orc, Inc. Security. This is Roc."

"Roc!" The voice on the other end released a long sigh. "Sorry to bother you after hours, old friend."

My mouth gaped. Not a client. "Jack?"

"I know it's been a while, but you know how crazy life gets."

I was too startled to reply. Jack might not have been a client of my personal security firm, but he had every reason to know my number. He was the one responsible for giving me my big break into providing orc security details for Hollywood celebrities. We'd both been young and new in LA, fast friends in a faster town. He'd become a talent agent and risen quickly in the ranks, while I'd struggled to find my place. That is, until Jack had recommended me as a bodyguard for one of his clients. One client had turned into many, until I had a staff of orcs providing security details for both the famous and infamous in Tinseltown and a business more successful than my most audacious dreams.

"It has been a while," I managed to say, as I pivoted away from my bedroom door. It had, in fact, been years since I'd heard from Jack directly. He'd gotten married, inherited step-kids, had more kids of his own, and drifted away from guys' nights out and casual hangs after work. I'd become more and more focused on my business until it was the smog-filled air I lived and breathed.

"That's my fault." Jack exhaled, and I could almost hear him rubbing a hand across his forehead like he used to do so often. "Between taking care of clients and my family, I dropped the ball."

I shook my head even though he couldn't see me. "No apologies needed." Then it struck me that he must have a reason for calling me after so long and so late. "Is everything okay? Hallie and the kids are okay?"

"Everyone's fine, although the kids aren't such little kids anymore." He barked out a pained laugh. "That's actually why I'm calling, Roc. I need a favor."

The worry in his voice made my spine straighten as I walked slowly back down the hallway. "Anything for you, Jack. You know that. I owe you everything."

"You don't owe me a thing." His voice was stern. "You earned your success. I just gave you a push in the right direction."

I knew we could argue all night, and Jack still wouldn't take the credit we both knew was his due. It didn't matter. Jack was my oldest friend, and I would never let him down. "Tell me what you need."

"I need you to be a personal bodyguard for a new actress. She's flying to a location shoot, and I want you to go with her."

I dragged one hand down the sides of my short beard as I passed through the kitchen. "You mean one of my guys, right? I don't do personal details anymore. It's a young orc's game."

Jack let out a bark of laughter. "You're younger than me, and I do *not* consider myself old. Besides, orcs age slower than humans and live longer."

I stole a look at my waist, which was no longer a washboard of muscles. Shifting from field work to managing my business from behind a desk had some definite drawbacks. "Of course, I'll do it if this is what you want, but why do you want me? I have a fleet of orc bodyguards who are the best in the business."

"I believe you, and I know your guys are the best. My talent agency still only uses Orc, Inc."

"Then it isn't my orcs. It's this actress." I walked toward my office. "You said she was new, so how much scrutiny could she be attracting?"

"She's on a hit TV show, and as the show's villain, she's been getting some unwanted attention."

I strode through the door of my office and took in the 180-degree view of the city lights spread out in front of me, a good reminder that Jack was a big part of why I had such a nice house with such a spectacular view. "Then maybe we should put a team on her."

"No team. I was barely able to convince her to have a single bodyguard for this trip. She isn't crazy about the security the studio has provided her so far—not your guys, clearly—and says they stifle her freedom. She hoped this location shoot would be a break from the LA spotlight and is not happy that I'm insisting on a bodyguard."

Clients who hated how security hampered their lives weren't new to me. It was one of the many reasons I'd stopped taking on personal assignments. Catering to the unreasonable whims of pampered starlets and cocky billionaires had taken its toll, as had trying to keep clients safe while they complained about the intrusive fans who had made them rich.

I sighed. "Your client isn't going to make this easy on me, is she?"

"She's not my client, Roc. The actress you'll be protecting is my daughter."

I squeezed my eyes closed. Fuck me.

TWO

Harlowe

T jammed another sweater into my suitcase and heaved the top over to close it, even though the bulge of clothes that spilled out the sides told me that it wasn't going to be easy. Sitting on the matte-silver hull of the roll-aboard brought the two sides a bit closer as I yanked at the zipper and cursed under my breath. I bounced up and down a few times, finally tugging the straining zipper all the way around and huffing out a breath. "Take that!"

I scraped a hand through my long hair. I was too young to be this angry, too young to be this burned out, too young to be sick of my life already. But I wasn't too young to be splashed across the covers of gossip magazines with salacious lies and the occasional painful truth buried inside the pages like precious gold flakes among so much dirt.

Standing, I glared at the suitcase sitting on the impossibly white carpet of my enormous closet, as if it were the reason for my anger. Anger that had been simmering inside me since I'd gotten the call from my dad telling me he was sending a bodyguard with me on my shoot.

"I don't need a bodyguard," I'd argued, as I'd paced the cool black tile of my kitchen, the only thing in my new house that wasn't white. "You're being ridiculous."

"I've seen the messages you've been getting on social media, Harlowe." My dad—technically my stepdad, but I'd always called him my dad since he'd raised me—had sounded genuinely worried.

I'd stalked from my open kitchen into the living room and flopped onto the armless sofa across from the armless chairs in the house that was too chic to contain any furniture with limbs. "People are upset that Zander and I broke up, but it will blow over."

I hated admitting that my entanglement with my co-star and love interest on our TV show—which everyone from my dad to my agent to my best friend had advised against—had blown up in my face. It didn't matter that he'd ended it. All fans saw was the show's temptress breaking Zander's heart on TV, so they decided that I was the villain in real life. Forget the fact that Zander was the one with the actual wandering eye. I couldn't prove that his other parts had wandered, but I had serious suspicions.

"Maybe, but I don't like the threats you've been getting. It only takes one..." His words had trailed off, but I didn't need him to finish the thought to know what he meant.

Although I claimed not to read social media comments, that was a lie. I'd seen what fans had posted about me, and I wasn't blind to the threats. Threats menacing enough for the studio to insist on extra security on set, and for me to be glad that I had a wall and gate around my house as well as a top-notch security system. I thought of the one fan who had made the scariest threats—and posted photos of himself outside my house—and I took a breath to steady my nerves.

I peered out the sliding glass doors that led to the terrace and the long pool overlooking the city. The gray haze huddled over LA was the only reason the view of so much glitz wasn't blinding in the mid-day, California sun. "This is supposed to be a relaxed location shoot. It's not even for the show. No one knows where I'm going or that I'm going."

"Not yet."

I released a tortured sigh I immediately regretted. I was twenty-three, but every time I talked to my dad, I felt like I was a little kid again. I got that he felt responsible for me, especially since it was his proximity to actors that had made me want to become one, but I hated that he made me feel like a child. Then I thought of what my scary fan had said he wanted to do to me, and a shiver slid down my spine. "Fine. One bodyguard, but he has to be low profile. I do not want to feel like I have a babysitter."

"I'm going to get you the best."

I stilled, a flicker of unease tickling my spine. I knew my dad used orc security exclusively, which I didn't mind. Having a hulking orc as a bodyguard usually scared off anyone who dared to approach you. I'd wished that the studio hired orcs more than once, since their human security details hadn't done much to dissuade the throngs of fans that hung around the studio gates. I imagined an orc bodyguard body slamming one of the guys who yelled out things he wanted to do to me, and I grinned.

Then my grin faded. As long as my dad didn't assign his friend Roc to protect me. Even the thought of the hot part-orc made my breath hitch in my throat. It had been years since I'd seen him, but I couldn't imagine that the green-skinned guy with dark hair he wore in a ponytail and serious don't-mess-with-me vibes had changed much. He'd given me butterflies when I was a teenager, and even now, the thought of him made my mouth go dry.

But Jack hadn't mentioned Roc in ages, and I hadn't even heard of the owner of Orc, Inc. providing security for anyone in a long time. He used to appear in the background of celebrity photos every so often, but that had stopped. As far as I knew, the guy could be retired.

"Only for this shoot." I matched my stern tone to my dad's. "This is not permanent."

He'd sighed, making me feel like I was fulfilling every stereotype of a spoiled starlet. "Fine."

"Everything will be okay, Dad." My voice softened. "I promise."

"Do you also promise to be nice to the bodyguard I'm sending? No running off or trying to ditch him."

I opened my mouth to protest before I realized he must have talked to the studio and heard about the times that Zander and I had given our security detail the slip. That had been more Zander's idea than mine, but no one believed that the golden boy was trouble. Not when I was around to blame for all the bad behavior.

I was too tired to argue anymore or explain my side of the story. "I promise."

Now that I stood in my closet, packed and ready to go, I regretted making that promise, especially since all I wanted to do was grab my suitcase and make a run for it. I eyed the silver case, wondering how far I could make it alone before I was spotted by an overeager fan and my photo ended up on social media. Maybe outside my front door?

The gate alarm jangled me from my pointless fantasies, and I grabbed my phone from a tufted bench, glancing quickly at the time and cursing that the orc bodyguard was a few minutes early. I shoved my phone into the pocket of my hoodie and released the handle of my suitcase so I could drag it from the closet, through my bedroom, and down the hall with me.

"If my fans could see me now," I muttered to myself with a laugh. I'm sure everyone would have expected Hollywood's newest diva to have a cadre of staff to do everything from pack to carry, but the truth was I despised having strangers underfoot. I'd always loved time alone, which was yet another reason I hated the idea of a bodyguard who would be with me all the time. Even if it meant dragging a suitcase so heavy it was giving my palm a blister.

The bell rang again, making me regret sending my assistant away early. "Chill out. I'm coming!"

I paused at the front double doors and gave a final glance at the Spartan interior of the house I'd only occupied for a few weeks, all white and glass and sharp edges. I wouldn't miss this place, even though it was exactly the kind of modern chic house everyone expected me to have. A location shoot in a quaint small town in the middle of nowhere was exactly what I needed, even if I did have to put up with a bodyguard tagging along.

Taking a quick glance at the monitor that showed me who was at the gate, I saw a driver in a limousine holding up studio credentials. No surprise there. The studio and my new bodyguard were apparently working together to coordinate my security and transportation.

I pressed the button to open the gate then made a quick dash to the kitchen to grab a can of water—eco-friendly so fans wouldn't see me with a single-use plastic bottle and call me out—before I ventured into the Southern California heat. A rap on the door told me that the limo hadn't wasted any time winding up the short, circular drive.

I opened the door and stepped aside so my orc bodyguard could come in and get my bag. "Just the one suitcase..." My words drifted into nothingness as my new bodyguard turned around. He might have been older and the slightest bit bulkier, but Roc had the same black hair pulled half up and dark scruff that I remembered so well. If I hadn't been holding onto the doorframe, I might have sagged to the floor. My childhood crush was my new bodyguard?

Fuck me.

THREE

Roc

I stole a sideways glance at the woman sitting next to me in the limousine. When Jack had said I would be protecting his daughter, I'd assumed he meant his younger daughter. I'd been fully prepared to escort a child star to a shoot that I'd thought would be with Disney or maybe Nickelodeon. I hadn't been prepared for the bombshell brunette who'd opened the door.

From her wide eyes and dangling jaw, I guessed she hadn't expected me either, but being part-orc, I was used to that kind of reception. She'd recovered quickly, stammering something about her dad not mentioning that I'd be her bodyguard before she practically bolted for the waiting vehicle.

How could I have forgotten Jack's older stepdaughter? I gave myself a mental scolding as I shook my head in disgust. It had been years since I'd seen Jack and his growing family, but my last memory of Harlowe had been of a slightly gawky, shy teenager. Nothing close to the long-limbed beauty whose jeans-clad legs were stretched in front of her as we rode to the airport.

I allowed my gaze to drift to her again, but this time I lingered. Her eyes were closed, and her head was tipped back on the headrest, so I could size her up without worry of being caught. Gone were the braces, gone were the purple-rimmed glasses, and gone were the plump cheeks. In their place were bow-shaped lips, long lashes fanned across creamy skin, and high cheekbones.

Also gone? My belief that I couldn't be rattled.

Even though my breath had steadied as I'd taken my time to wheel her suitcase behind her to the limo, my heart still felt as if it had been squeezed like a rubber stress ball. I jerked my head away and closed my own eyes, letting my fingers drum gently on the leather seat. I needed to get my head in the game and my mind focused on the job. It didn't matter what my client looked like or that seeing her had been akin to jamming a metal prong in a light socket.

You've been too isolated, I told myself. The only reason you reacted was because it's been so long since you've encountered a beautiful woman in real life.

I huffed out a breath. That was it. I'd shut myself off from the world for too long, and this was what happened. I would adjust to being around humans again. My gut clenched as I thought about the coming week. I had no choice.

"I should have known."

I opened my eyes to find Harlowe staring at me, her blue eyes narrowed. Had her eyes always been so blue, or had I simply not paid attention to her because she was a teenager? I fought to keep my gaze locked on her face. She certainly wasn't a teenager anymore. Quick mental math told me she must be in her early twenties, not that it mattered. She was still Jack's stepdaughter and my client. Both made her entirely off-limits. Being my friend's daughter made her radioactive.

Her eyes narrowed more, and one eyebrow arched in question. She'd said something. I cleared my throat and folded my arms across my chest to give myself an extra beat to remember. "You should have known what?"

She fluttered a hand at me, her pink-tipped fingers dancing through the air. "My dad said he was hiring the best bodyguard for me. I should have guessed that he'd get you."

Her tone was accusatory, but I didn't know how this was my fault or why Jack hiring me to guard her was a bad thing. "He called in a favor."

Her brows leapt higher. "I'm a favor?"

I scowled, not enjoying how rapidly this conversation was unraveling. Where was the shy girl who'd run from the room when I appeared? Where was the coltish teen who'd snuck peeks at me around the door frame before her mother shooed her away? Grown-up Harlowe didn't seem to back down from anything, which did nothing for my pattering heart rate. Orcs—even ones who weren't full-blooded—loved nothing more than a challenge. Not that she was a challenge I welcomed. "I do not personally provide security anymore. I have a sizable team who handles clients."

"But my dad wanted you to *handle* me personally?"

I doubted anyone handled Harlowe, but I pressed my lips together to keep from saying that and felt the bite of my sharp tusks. Instead of answering her, I asked my own question. "Jack told me you don't want security. Why not?"

She sighed and her shoulders sagged as if all the air had been let out of them. "You mean, why don't I want someone dogging my steps every moment of every day?" She held up a hand. "And don't say that it's all part of being a celebrity. I'm fully aware of what I signed up for when I decided to become an actress, but I did not sign up for harassment."

"I would never say that. The reason I'm here is so you won't have to deal with anyone bothering you."

She choked back a brittle laugh. "What if having you around bothers me?"

I ignored the flash of pain that had been my constant companion when it came to acceptance in the human world. I couldn't help it if Harlowe didn't like the idea of having an orc around. I'd made a promise to her father. A promise I wasn't willing to break, even if it ripped open every tenuously scabbed-over wound. "My presence is non-negotiable. I'm here at your father's request to keep you safe. It would be helpful if you cooperated, but I will do my job regardless."

I ground out the words through a tight jaw, only stealing a glance at her as the limousine glided to a stop on the tarmac of the private airstrip. Harlowe's expression was stricken.

"I didn't mean—"

"You do not need to like me or like the fact that I'm here. I'm not here to be your friend or to make you comfortable. I am here to protect you." The door opened, and I stepped from the car before the woman could respond.

It didn't matter what she said. I'd promised to keep her safe. End of story.

I slid on a pair of dark sunglasses to shield my eyes from the bright sun as I scanned the tarmac, which was deserted save for the sleek, private jet steps away. When Harlowe emerged, she'd slipped on a pair of sunglasses as well—big, oversized ones that concealed the top half of her face. She didn't spare me a glance as she strode past me and toward the white plane, her shoulders thrown back and her chin raised.

I exhaled, almost relieved that she so clearly despised me. It would be easier to do my job if there was nothing between us, and if Harlowe's reaction to me was any indication, the only feelings she had for me were laden with irritation.

"Just the way I like it," I growled as I grabbed her suitcase and followed her onto the plane.

FOUR

Harlowe

This was bad. I fastened my seat belt across my lap even as my hands trembled and then tucked my fingers under my legs to keep Roc from seeing how much he'd unnerved me. Even though he sat across the aisle, he was facing me, and I could sense his gaze sliding to me every minute or so.

Why did it have to be *him*? Of all the bodyguards in the world—all the orcs in the world—why did my dad have to hire the one who'd been the stuff of my teenage fantasies? Not that my dad had known that I'd been fascinated by his part-orc friend, or that I'd eagerly anticipated the nights Roc would come over for dinner or to hang out by our pool on a sunny afternoon. It hadn't helped that the orc had been tall and buff. With his long, dark hair and matching scruff, he'd been like catnip to a girl who liked the idea of a bad boy without any of the consequences.

So much for no consequences, I thought, as I made a point not to look his way, even though I hadn't shed my sunglasses inside the plane. The moment I'd seen Roc, I'd turned into an idiot. My face flamed with heat as I remembered his jaw ticking when I'd told him that having him around bothered me.

That hadn't been a lie. His presence did bother me, just not in the way that he thought. What he probably thought was that I hated him, which made me twitch in the buttery, leather seat and want to blurt out a half-assed apology.

I could do it, I thought, as I twisted my head to take in the small interior of the plane that was bathed in beige. There was no one else on board. Not even a flight attendant, since our flight was short and more people on board meant more chances for my location to be revealed.

I opened my mouth and then clamped it closed just as swiftly. What would I say? *I didn't mean that having you around bothered me in a bad way. You bother me in a good way.* Sure, Harlowe, that wouldn't be awkward to explain at all.

No way was I going to confess *that* to my childhood crush, not when just looking at him made my stomach do a backflip. It was one thing to see a past crush and realize that you were young and silly to ever have liked him. It was another to have all those old feelings wash over you just as powerfully as if no time had passed.

It didn't help that Roc looked almost exactly like he had a decade ago. Maybe he wasn't as lean anymore, but if it was possible, he looked even sexier now that he wasn't in his twenties. It was common knowledge that orcs aged slower than humans, but Roc's maturity only added to his appeal. Now that I'd been around him for even a short amount of time, my costar who was also twenty-three seemed like a child.

"Zander *is* a child," I said under my breath as the plane rumbled down the runway.

Roc snapped his head to me, but I pretended like I hadn't spoken as I slid my hands from under my legs to grip the armrests of my seat.

Get your shit together, Harlowe. You are going to a location shoot and Roc is your bodyguard. Nothing else. Like he said, he isn't your friend, and he definitely isn't interested in being anything more. Not after what you said to him.

I used the roar of takeoff to mask a groan, leaning back in the seat as the plane lifted off the ground. My stomach dropped like it always did when the plane caught air, but then we were up.

Besides, I told myself, Roc is your dad's friend, and Jack would flip his shit if he knew you had a crush on the bodyguard he was trusting to keep you safe.

No big deal. It's a short trip, a quick shoot, and then the hot orc would be out of my life. That thought sent a pang of sadness through me, but I flicked it away like a pesky insect. What did I really think could happen? Did I legit think that Roc would fulfill every secret fantasy I'd had about him? He'd made it clear that he was only with me as a favor to my dad. He probably still thought of me as an annoying kid anyway. Not that I hadn't given him plenty of reason to think the worst of me.

The plane leveled out, and I glanced at the orc again. His arms might be folded over his chest and his eyes shut, but I noticed that his hands were fisted so tightly that I could see the white of his knuckles through the muddy green of his skin. Was it possible he didn't like flying?

Just as I was about to ask him if he was okay, my phone buzzed in the pocket of my hoodie. Crap. Had I left it on?

I yanked it out and peered at the screen, releasing a

breath when I saw my agent's name. If I didn't answer, he'd just continue to call. I wouldn't put it past him to appear outside the plane's window. "Hey, Grant."

"Harlowe." Why did he always sound out of breath? "I'm glad you answered—"

"You know I'm on the way to the shoot, right?"

"Of course, I know. I arranged it all with the studio. I wanted to grab you before you started shooting. I just negotiated a new deal for you."

I sat up. "With...?"

"The show wants you to sign for another three seasons." The words rushed from him like he was being charged by the second. "Isn't that fantastic?"

"Three seasons?" I couldn't keep the dread from my voice. Three more seasons meant I was locked into three years of awkwardness with Zander, three years of playing the same character, three years of being a villain fans loved to hate.

"It's a lot of money, Har."

I bristled at the nickname he'd given me without asking. I hated people who shortened everyone's names because they thought it meant they were in some sort of inner circle. "I can't make that kind of decision now."

"Tick-tock, sweetie. This deal has an expiration date."

You have an expiration date, I thought. I rubbed a hand over my forehead at the childish comeback I forced myself to swallow. I'd definitely spent too much time with my twelve-year-old sister, who was the queen of sassy backtalk.

"Listen, Grant. We're heading into some turbulence. I appreciate you negotiating this deal and my answer is—" I disconnected the call, turned off my phone, and dropped it on the empty seat beside me.

When I looked up, I caught Roc eyeing me. Before he wiped his expression and turned to peer out the window, I could have sworn that he'd been grinning at me.

More delusions, I said to myself as I tore my gaze from him. The last person Roc would be smiling at was the client who was a brat to him.

CHAPTER
FIVE

Roc

Why had I agreed to this job? I let out a guttural sound as I remembered saying yes before I knew there would be a tiny plane involved.

I hated tiny planes. I hated their low ceilings. I hated their impossibly cramped bathrooms. I hated that I was stuck on one with a client who wanted to be anywhere but with me.

"Doesn't matter," I husked to myself, my words drowned by the growl of the engines. I'd promised to do Jack a favor and that was what I was going to do, no matter how much I repulsed his stepdaughter.

Harlowe said something I couldn't catch over the noise of takeoff, and I swiveled my head to see if she was talking to me. It was clear she wasn't. She averted her gaze and tipped her head back as the plane barreled down the runway and lifted into the air.

Now that the plane was airborne, I released a breath.

I might not be a full-blooded orc, but that didn't mean I was any less attached to the ground. Orcs were mountain-dwellers, hulking creatures not intended to leave the earth, a fact I was reminded of every time I boarded a metal tube meant to hurtle through the sky.

Three-quarter orc, I reminded myself, as if made a difference to anyone but full orcs who'd always eyed my smaller tusks and less bulky stature with derision. It didn't make a difference to the pretty human sitting across the aisle. She'd made it clear that she didn't want me around.

I chanced a peek out the window as we climbed toward the clouds, then I forced myself to keep my gaze inside the plane, crossing my arms over my chest and closing my eyes. There was no one else in the compact cabin but me and Harlowe, so I didn't need to be on alert, even though it was impossible to fully relax when I was working.

The steady hum of the engines told me that we'd reached cruising altitude, but Harlowe's voice snapped me from my steady breathing.

"Hey, Grant." The tone of her voice told me that Grant wasn't a love interest. "You know I'm on the way to the shoot, right?"

I opened one eye to see her cross one leg over the other and pump her top foot, as she gnawed on her bottom lip and listened with her iPhone pressed to her ear.

"Three seasons?"

Now I opened both eyes and watched her frown and her foot jiggle. Everything about her body language told me that she wasn't happy with whatever Grant was telling her. A strange, protective sensation washed over me, which wasn't unusual, considering that I'd been hired to protect her. What was unusual was my overwhelming desire to snatch the phone from her ear and stop this Grant from upsetting my client. Harlowe wasn't in any kind of physical danger, but my fingers tingled with the desire to shield her from everything.

Not your job, Roc. Stick to what you were hired to do.

Harlowe's back visibly stiffened as she switched the phone to her other ear. "I can't make that kind of decision now." She rubbed her free hand over her forehead as if trying to smooth out invisible wrinkles before she huffed out a breath. "Listen, Grant. We're heading into some turbulence. I appreciate you negotiating this deal and my answer is—"

Harlowe disconnected the call, powered down her phone and tossed it in the seat beside her. I couldn't help grinning at her tactic, even though I didn't want her to know I was amused by her, or that I was listening in on her conversation. When she darted a glance at me, I wiped the smile from my face and cut my gaze out the window.

My skin still buzzed as if there was an active threat, which was insane since we were thousands of feet in the air. No one could get to Harlowe, especially since she'd turned off her phone, so why was I vibrating with rage? Was it because I'd detected a tremble of fear in her voice? Was it because I'd felt her tension as if it were my own? Was it because she was so small and delicate compared to me? Or was it because Harlowe affected me like no one had before, and the thought of her experiencing any distress made me want to hurl something?

I ground my teeth and attempted to banish thoughts of the human from my mind, a near impossibility since she was sitting across from me.

It doesn't matter. She's the client. You're the bodyguard. And she's Jack's stepdaughter.

That did it. Besides, Harlowe was a gorgeous Hollywood star, the kind of woman who had hot, hard-bodied men falling at her feet. An orc who was quickly approaching both forty and a dad bod didn't stand a chance. Not that I would even take a shot at someone like her.

Before I could laugh out loud at the prospect of me with Harlowe, the plane spluttered—then dropped.

CHAPTER
SIX

Harlowe

"What the hell?" I clutched the armrests of my seat and locked eyes on Roc as the plane's engines made sounds that were less than reassuring.

Whatever image of calm he'd been exuding vanished, and he unbuckled his seat belt and bolted to his feet, bracing his large hands on the ceiling to keep himself steady. "Stay here. I will check with the pilots."

"As if I can go anywhere," I muttered to no one as he disappeared into the cockpit.

I squeezed my eyes shut and tried not to think about plummeting to the ground. This is what I get, I thought. This is what happens when you wish to be a successful actress, and you get everything you ever wanted and a whole lot that you didn't.

"I'm going to be like all those famous people who died in private planes," I said out loud, not caring that there was no one to hear me. Actually, it was better that I was alone. That way I could say whatever I wanted, and Roc wouldn't think I was crazy.

A manic laugh slipped from my lips. Why did I care what the hot orc thought about me if we were all going to die? My mind instantly went to my dad who'd called in a favor to get his orc friend to protect me and then to my mom. They'd both be devastated. So would my sisters. Thinking about my family made a hard lump lodge in my throat, and I shook my head as tears threatened to fall.

"Stop it. You're being dramatic."

How many times had my mother said that exact thing when I was growing up? Of course, I'd been dramatic. It wasn't a shock when I'd gone into acting after a lifetime of overreacting.

A pang of regret shot through me. I hoped my family would remember the good things about me and not just that I'd been a teenage drama queen. My thoughts shifted to my best friends from high school, the ones I'd fallen out of touch with once I'd started getting booked for roles. I'd always thought I'd have time to reconnect with them.

My heart was pounding so hard I was afraid I'd stroke out before the plane crashed, as image after image of family and friends flashed through my mind. Then I thought of broad-shouldered Roc standing on my doorstep dressed in black with a strand of hair falling loose across his forehead. Even though he made my palms sweaty and my mouth dry, I was glad he was the one who was with me.

I jumped at something closing over my clenched hand on the armrest. Roc was strapping in next to me, his big green hand over mine.

"Is this it?"

He gave his head a brusque shake. "The plane is not going to crash, but we do need to make an emergency landing."

My pattering heart stuttered for a moment. "An emergency landing? At an airstrip?"

He shook his head. "There is no airport close enough."

Great. We were landing somewhere without an airstrip. "Isn't that the same as crashing?"

Roc's brow was furrowed and his jaw tight, but he squeezed my hand. "No. We will be fine."

I didn't dare look out the window because I had a feeling knowing wouldn't help. I would know soon enough if it was forest, mountains, or open plains.

"Promise?" The second the plea left my mouth, I hated how childish it sounded. If the orc hadn't thought I was still a kid before, he would now.

But Roc didn't laugh, didn't scoff, didn't even flinch. "I promise."

My hand beneath his trembled like it was a trapped creature trying to escape, but he didn't let go and the warmth of his skin seeped into mine. Instead of making my flesh buzz as it had before, his touch sent soothing pulses through me. I was able to match my breaths to his slow, even ones as the plane descended.

"When it's time to brace, I will cover your body with mine." Roc didn't look at me as he said this, and his tone didn't invite discussion.

He was willing to risk his life to save mine, and all because he'd had the bad luck to owe my dad a favor. My gut churned with shame at how I'd treated him. "I'm sorry."

He twisted his head to meet my gaze. "For what?"

"I've been a jerk, but it has nothing to do with you. I'm mad that I have to have a bodyguard period."

"You don't have to say that. I understand that not everyone welcomes orc—"

"No, really. It's true." I swiveled my hand under his so that I could interlace our fingers. "I promise."

His pupils flared dark for a beat before the plane jerked and the pilot's voice boomed over the intercom. "Brace for impact!"

Roc shoved my head between my legs and threw his body over mine as the plane slammed down with teeth-rattling force.

CHAPTER
SEVEN

Roc

The silence that settled over me was like a shroud, blocking out all sound but the ringing in my ears. The rumbling of the plane's engines had stopped. The screaming of the metal hull being dragged across treetops had stopped. The pilot's bellowed warnings had stopped. The only thing I was sure hadn't stopped was the trembling of the woman beneath me.

I peeled myself off Harlowe, aware that I'd been practically laying on top of her. "Are you hurt?"

Her hands were interlaced behind her head as she remained curled over her legs, eyelids squeezed so tight they appeared to be glued together. I gave her small frame a quick assessment. No blood. No bruises. No unusually bent limbs.

The grateful gush of breath from my own throat startled me. She hadn't been hurt in the crash. Scared, definitely, but not hurt or killed.

"Harlowe?" My tone was more insistent now, and I bent over her with a hand on her back.

She jerked up, her eyes wide as her gaze darted around the plane. "We're alive?"

"Unless we both got a low-rent version of heaven." Now that I was certain my protectee was safe, I unhooked my seatbelt and scanned the interior. Aside from overhead bins dangling open and a few bags strewn across the floor, the cabin appeared intact. I retrieved my cell phone, frowning at the absence of any reception.

I stood and glanced at the cockpit door. Since the captain had yelled for us to brace, I hadn't heard his voice again. I made my way toward the faux-wood door, pushing it open and steeling myself for what I might find.

Both the pilot and co-pilot were upright in their seats and in the process of unfastening their restraints and rubbing their necks. I peered beyond them to a field of tall, green stalks that were partially flattened around the nose of the plane.

"You landed us in a corn field?"

The silver-haired pilot glanced at me. "We got lucky."

"The corn didn't," his copilot added, groaning as he removed the belt crossing his shoulders.

"Where are we?" I could assume that we weren't near LA, but I had no clue where there was farmland like this.

"Our navigation went out before our engines, but we should be in Oregon."

Oregon? I cut another look at the field. When I thought of Oregon, I imagined coastline and hipsters, not farmland.

"How is the other passenger?" the pilot asked without taking his gaze from the controls.

"Unhurt but shaken."

He grunted and scraped a hand through his close-cropped hair. "I'll open the doors. We should disembark until we know the plane isn't a fire hazard."

It hadn't occurred to me that the plane could still be dangerous, but now that I thought about it, the idea of staying in a metal box filled with fuel and malfunctioning equipment did not appeal. I left the cockpit and strode back to the small interior of the plane where Harlow still sat in precisely the same position she'd been in when I'd left.

I crouched in front of her and unhooked her seatbelt. "We need to leave the plane."

Her dazed expression snapped to me, and her fast breath hitched. "Why?"

I took her hand and pulled her to standing. "It isn't safe to remain on board."

She nodded as I scooped her shoulder bag and carry-on from the floor and then grabbed her roller-board suitcase from the overhead bin. The co-pilot had opened the door of the jet and lowered the stairs, nodding to us as I led Harlowe to the exit.

She paused at the top, glanced outside then looked back at me. "It's a field."

"Better than a freezing lake," the co-pilot muttered behind us.

"I'll go first." I stepped down the stairs and jumped from the last one to a patch of flattened stalks. I dropped her bags, turned, and extended my arms. "I'll catch you."

With a reluctant glance behind her, Harlowe descended the stairs, took a breath and leapt. I caught her by the waist and lowered her to the ground, forcing myself not to dwell on how close her body was to mine as her breasts nearly brushed my nose. I kept my lips pressed together to keep from emitting a growl and set her down gently in front of me.

I pivoted back to the jet, expecting the pilots to join us. The co-pilot followed, jumping down from the stairs and making his way around the bruised hull of the white jet as he shook his head. Once he'd made a complete circle and returned to the stairs, his brow wasn't as wrinkled.

"No fire. That's good."

"So now what?" Harlowe asked. Her rapid breathing and shocked expression had faded, replaced by a look of irritation.

"The captain and I need to try arrange a rescue and salvage, but that might take a while."

Harlowe looked to me. "Should we wait here?"

My gut told me that we should not stay in a crashed plane, especially since it would be nighttime soon. I shook my head. "This is a cultivated field, which means it's someone's farm."

She snapped her fingers. "Which means there has to be a farmer."

Hopefully, one who wasn't livid that our plane had scorched a trail through his field.

Harlowe twisted her head from one side to the other before scooping up her bag and carry-on from the ground. "Which way do we walk?"

I eyed the flattened stalks behind us and the dense ones in front of us. "The easy way."

With a reassurance to the co-pilot that we would send help when we found it, I led the way back through the path of battered crops dragging her small rolling suitcase behind me. Harlowe walked silently by my side, the only sound that of our feet crunching the crushed plants. I usually welcomed quiet, but this silence hung leaden between us, the corridor of remaining stalks buffeting us and keeping everything unsaid from escaping.

"Thank you." Harlowe's voice interrupted our rhythmic footfall.

I slid my gaze to her, but she walked with her head facing forward and her chin lifted high. "For...?"

"Saving me. You covered my body with yours. You didn't have to do that."

"I did."

She let loose an impatient moan. "I've had bodyguards before, Roc. None of them would take a bullet for me."

"I am not like them."

She tipped her head to meet my gaze, studying me for a beat. "No, you aren't."

Before I could wonder about the various ways she was comparing me to her human bodyguards—they weren't green, didn't have tusks, didn't have a violent streak—she smiled shyly and looked away. My heart squeezed, blood rushing in my ears just like it had when I'd cocooned my body over hers as the plane had gone down. But this time it wasn't the potent cocktail of fear and the need to protect that fired my blood.

She'd smiled at me. Not the kind of tight smile I was accustomed to receiving when humans wanted to pretend they were accepting but were fighting back the urge to run or scream. It had been a warm smile that sent heat buzzing across my skin.

Maybe she wasn't like most humans. She'd told me that it wasn't me that she'd objected to but the presence of a bodyguard in the first place. I had to accept the possibility that she wasn't opposed to me because I was an orc. It was hard to let go of the assumption that humans feared me since I'd found it to be true again and again. But

Harlowe wasn't like most humans I'd known, and she was entirely different from the previous famous actors I'd protected.

Of course, she is. She's Jack's daughter.

Jack's daughter. That truth doused my heat like a torrent of freezing water. It didn't matter if Harlowe wasn't like other humans or other actors or other women. It didn't matter if she had no issue with me being an orc or even if she had an orc fetish. She was still my friend's daughter, and I was her bodyguard.

"Hold it right there, orc."

I froze, berating myself for losing focus and practically walking into the grizzled man holding a shotgun. I lifted my hands as Harlowe stilled, her own hands going into the air.

"Our plane crashed," she said before I could explain. "We need help."

The old man lowered his weapon and eyed her, his gaze shifting to the path behind us. "I can see that you crashed into my field."

"I'm very sorry." Harlowe's voice sounded so sincere and apologetic I no longer wondered why she was finding success as an actress. "Our plane malfunctioned, and we couldn't make it to an airstrip. We'll reimburse you for your crop."

The farmer grunted and dropped his shotgun to his side. "You're lucky you aren't dead. You weren't flying it, were you?"

Harlowe shook her head. "Our pilots stayed with the plane. We came looking for help."

The man's eyes narrowed as he stared at her. "You look familiar." Then he grinned. "You're on that show my wife watches." Without waiting for her confirmation, he spun on his heel. "You'd better come on in. The missus will have my hide if I leave you standing in the field."

The old man seemed harmless enough now that he wasn't leveling a gun at us, but I couldn't relax. Not yet. Not until I got Harlowe to safety.

CHAPTER
EIGHT

Harlowe

"I can't believe Harlowe Watts is sitting in my kitchen." The woman with tightly permed, unnaturally black hair swatted her husband with a dish towel. "Can you, Gerry?"

Gerry grunted, but his wife wasn't dissuaded by his lack of an answer. She leaned against the countertop and shook her head as she stared at me. "I just can't believe it."

The woman wasn't what I would have thought was my target demographic, but the celebrity magazines jammed in the magazine rack by the Laz-E-Boy recliner closest to the kitchen told me that Brenda followed Hollywood gossip closer than I did. I curled a hand around the glass of iced tea sweating on the plastic place mat and eyed the plate of buttery cinnamon crumbs that had been a wedge of coffee cake before I'd devoured it.

The house carried the mingled scents of a freshly baked

cake and lemon furniture polish, which was an improvement over the aroma of manure and fertilizer that lingered outside the farmhouse.

"Thanks again for letting us use your phone." I cut my gaze to Roc, who'd made the calls to my dad and my manager. "I'm sure we'll be out of your hair as soon as..."

"We can find a way to get to the nearest airport," he finished for me.

What? I mouthed. How were we supposed to get to an airport without a functioning plane?

"They've booked another plane to get us the rest of the way to the shoot, but by the time they send a driver to get us and take us there, the plane won't be available." Roc kept his voice low as if the Gerry and Brenda weren't opening listening and hanging on every word. At least, Brenda was. Gerry seemed almost bored by our arrival, once he'd determined that we weren't aliens or government agents.

"You need a ride?" Brenda smacked her husband with the red-striped towel again. "We've got a truck we don't ever use anymore, don't we, Gerry?"

Gerry jerked his head up, as if he'd just that moment realized his wife was talking to him, which was probably the case. "What truck?"

Brenda released a long-suffering sigh. "The red one. You don't mind if these two borrow it, do you?"

"Borrow it?"

Gerry seemed to be several steps behind the conversation as he rubbed his head and struggled to catch up.

"I'm sure they'll bring it back." Brenda beamed at me. "After all, this is Harlowe Watts. I'm sure a big star like her doesn't have any need to keep your ratty old truck."

"Ratty?" Now Gerry straightened. "Just 'cause it needs some new paint—"

"It runs fine even though it don't look like much." Brenda walked toward the screen door and snatched a set of keys from a hook on the wall. She shot a look at her husband before he could voice his protest, then she smiled at me. "You keep it as long as you need it, hon."

Roc stood and took the keys, which made Brenda's eyes widen for a beat. It was obvious they didn't get many orcs around here. At least, not part-orcs who dressed in expensive suits.

"We'll get it back to you as soon as we can." I took a final sip of tea and stood. "You have my word."

Brenda flapped a hand at me, her eyes misting as she yanked me toward her into a fierce hug.

"Let the poor girl go before you smother her," Gerry said under his breath. Then he strode to the screen door and jerked his head toward the barn that sat across from the house. "Come on. I'll show you the truck."

I followed behind Roc once I'd dislodged myself from Brenda's grasp. "Don't we need to check on the pilots?"

"I'll fetch them," Gerry said before Roc could respond, proving that he had selective hearing when it came to listening to his wife. "Unless you need to take them with you now."

Roc grunted his version of a no as he grabbed my rolling suitcase from where he'd left it outside the kitchen door. "We need to get to the replacement flight, but the private jet company is sending a repair crew here and equipment so they can tow the plane."

Gerry made a rough noise on the back of his throat. "That should be great for my field."

"They'll reimburse you," I said quickly before Roc could say something, which, from the dark expression on his face wasn't going to be as gracious. "I promise that you'll be well compensated."

Gerry grumbled and nodded as he led us across the gravel driveway to a barn built from silvered wood that had warped over the years. He pulled open the door, which complained with a loud squeak, to reveal a truck that had probably been red at some point in its long life. Now it was rusted and battered with only glimpses of paint clinging to its exterior.

"She's got enough gas to get you to town." He slapped the front hood, and I held my breath that it wouldn't collapse from the impact. "Take a right out of the farm and go straight until you hit the traffic light."

"Then what?" Roc asked as he walked around the truck with one eyebrow cocked so high it threatened to vanish within his hairline.

"Then you're there." Gerry looked at him like he'd asked the most absurd question in the world. "The town's got the only traffic light around."

I hoped that the one-light town had a gas station and cell service. "Thanks again. We'll get your truck back to you in one piece."

Roc emitted a guttural sound that told me I might be making promises about the truck he couldn't keep, but he didn't say anything as he put my suitcase in the flat bed and opened the passenger door for me.

"I guess I ought to thank you." Gerry cleared his throat. "Brenda will be talking about nothing but meeting you for years, which means she won't have as much time to nag me."

"Don't mention it." I managed to give the surly old man a smile as Roc closed the door and made his way around the front of the truck, got inside, and turned the key in the ignition. I held my breath as the truck spluttered and coughed before the engine caught.

Gerry stepped back as we rolled from the barn and bumped down the uneven gravel drive, turning right onto the paved road. I peered into the side view mirror and saw Brenda hanging from the kitchen door and waving. I rolled down my window and waved back then rolled the window up and looked over at Roc.

He had both hands on the steering wheel and his profile was stern as he kept his gaze on the road. Suddenly, I was overcome with the urge to laugh, and I slapped a hand over my mouth to muffle the giggles that bubbled up in my throat.

"What?" He turned toward me as I collapsed in a fit of laughter.

"You." I waved a hand at him. "This." I circled my hand to encompass the interior of the musty truck. "They don't fit."

He watched me laugh, his own lips twitching at the corners. "You don't think I look like a truck kind of guy?"

Roc's chic, black suit and his effortless bad-boy vibe did not mesh at all with the country vibe of a truck that was probably older than me. "Not even a little bit. You're way too hot and badass for a rusted truck."

As soon as the words had spilled from my lips, I regretted them. *Please, please, please don't pick up on—*

"You think I'm hot?"

So much for hoping he wouldn't pick up on that. I tried to laugh it off. "Come on, Roc. You know you're hot. Don't you notice the way women look at you?"

"Women stare at me because I'm part orc."

Did he really think that was why he attracted attention? Sure, maybe some people were surprised, but it wasn't like monsters were a total surprise anymore. Not all of them mingled with humans, but orcs were not unheard of in LA. I suspected most women who gawked at Roc were reacting to the fact that he was a genuinely handsome orc who radiated raw sex appeal. "I've got news for you. That's not why they're staring."

He looked at me like I'd sprouted a nose from my forehead. "I don't fit in with the human world."

My laughter died away as I watched him tighten his hands on the steering wheel. "Is that why you disappeared? You think you don't fit in?"

"It is not what I think. It's the truth."

"The only thing I know to be true is that you stopped coming around, and my dad thought he'd done something wrong." My throat squeezed as I remembered asking about Roc when I was younger. "I thought you were staying away because you didn't like us anymore."

He swung his head to me. "You didn't do anything wrong, and my feelings for your family have never changed."

My heart pounded as I met his eyes, and the question popped out before I could think better of it. "What about your feelings for me?"

"What?" He blinked a few times before glancing back to the road and slamming on the brakes so hard we both lurched forward. I braced my hand on the dashboard and looked up. We'd reached the stop light.

CHAPTER
NINE

Roc

We'd found the town, its single traffic light glaring red, as I pressed my foot into the brake so hard I feared it might break through the rusted floor of the truck. My breathing was ragged, my palms gripping the steering wheel were sweaty, and my heart pounded. Why had Harlowe asked about my feelings for her?

I couldn't have feelings for her. She was my protectee, she was my friend's daughter, and she was a human. All of that made her off-limits.

I slowly uncoiled my fingers and eased my foot off the brake as the light turned green, letting the truck roll through the intersection and into the downtown that was so compact I could probably have passed through it without hitting the gas once. There was a town square that had seen more prosperous days—the gazebo was shedding paint and the bushes around it were brown—and squat, brick buildings lining the street that curled around the square.

At the far end, I spotted a gas station with a circular drive, and I rolled the truck into it and beside the single pump before I killed the engine. "We found the town."

Harlowe made a noise I couldn't decipher as she jerked open the passenger door and slid out, slamming the door behind her with such force I expected it to fall off its hinges. I sat for another moment to catch my breath and think about what she'd said. Had Jack really blamed himself when I'd stopped coming around?

I'd never explained why I'd become more of a recluse because I'd never planned it. My aversion to humans had come about slowly, but it would be fair to say that the more wealthy, dismissive clients I worked with, the less I wanted to expose myself to their derision.

The rich and powerful of Hollywood were more than happy to use orc protection, but that didn't mean they had any problem treating me and my orc bodyguards like the lesser creatures they believed us to be. To be fair, they probably treated everyone like that, but I felt it more keenly because I'd always been treated as an "other."

But not by Jack.

Guilt gnawed at me. Jack had never looked at me differently or treated me differently, so why had I painted him with the same broad, orc-fearing strokes? Had it been easier to lump all humans in together? If that was the case, it didn't make me any better than the people who shrank from the sight of green skin and tusks.

I watched Harlowe walk around the front of the truck and twist her back from side to side before putting her hands on her hips to survey the small town. I owed Jack an apology, but first, I had to finish the job he'd entrusted to me. Unfortunately, that job was the single biggest distraction I'd ever encountered.

I wrenched open the car door, careful not to tear it off, and slid from the truck. I closed the door, causing the metal to rattle and threaten to come apart. When it didn't, I huffed out a relieved breath and prodded open the vehicle's gas flap and unscrewed the cap. I took the fuel nozzle from the pump, shoved it into the truck, and squeezed it to start the gas pumping.

The pump stalled for a beat before the numbers started to lazily flip to indicate that gas was flowing. Even though the air carried the aroma of gasoline, it didn't smell of manure, which I counted as a good thing. But the town looked almost as abandoned as the farm we'd left, with half of the glass-front storefronts boarded up and only a few stragglers walking about.

"Are we sure this is a town?" Harlowe whispered as she walked up to me, breaking the silence between us.

I caught her eye and was grateful to see her grinning. I jerked my head toward the intersection behind us. "It does have the traffic light."

"Good thing neither of us sneezed going through, or we might have missed it." Harlowe shook her head. "It's hard to think there are places this deserted so close to LA."

"Two hours by plane isn't very close."

"Still." She flicked a hand through her hair. "LA is so busy and clogged, but there is so much open land out here. I get why people choose to live away from LA."

"You do?" I'd seen her splashy house with a pool overlooking the city. It was hardly a small-town vibe.

She closed her eyes as she inhaled. "Do you hear that?"

I paused, straining to pick up any sounds aside from the rhythmically flipping numbers of the gas pump. Aside from the pump, there was nothing to break the quiet. No car horns. No jets overhead. No jackhammering from construction. "There's nothing."

"Exactly." She opened her eyes and her smile widened. "Back in LA, there's nonstop motion and chaos. This is a place that forward momentum forgot, and I'm here for it."

I understood how easy it was to embrace quiet. Quiet was why I lived far enough from the city that I couldn't hear its madness. But I also knew that up-and-coming actresses couldn't retreat to the country if they wanted to make it big. Idaho ranches were for stars who'd made their names and their money.

"You do remember that we're passing through?" I asked. "They're still expecting you on-set."

Harlowe's smile dropped, and she spared me a withering look. "I remember. I know we can't stay here. I was just saying that I get why people do." She shrugged. "But, who knows? Maybe being this remote would drive me crazy after a while."

I scanned the cracked sidewalks and dented metal awnings shading shuttered stores. "There's a difference between remote and deserted."

"Good point." Harlowe patted my arm, her fingers barely touching me. "This town does give off abandoned-after-a-string-of-unsolved-murders energy."

I raised an eyebrow at her, trying to ignore the lingering heat from her hand on my sleeve. She caught my expression and laughed. "So, I listen to too many true crime podcasts. Shoot me."

"That wasn't in your *People Magazine* profile."

She tilted her head at me and scrunched her lips to one side as she studied me. "You read my profile in *People*?"

I was grateful that my green skin kept me from revealing flushed cheeks. "I always research my clients."

"Well, a *People Magazine* profile written by my publicist isn't going to tell you much about me. Besides, you already know me. More than most people, at least."

"That was when you were a child."

She held up a finger. "A teenager, thank you very much."

She'd seemed like a child to me, although in the ensuing decade she was very far from what I remembered. "It was a long time ago."

"And who's fault is that?" Her tone was sharp, telling me she wasn't going to let this go.

"Mine. It was all mine."

She tapped one toe on the gas-stained pavement as if waiting for me to continue.

"The bigger my business became—all thanks to your father—the more I was reminded how different I was from my wealthy human clients. After a few movie stars who insisted on calling me Orc, usually while snapping a finger, I decided to let my staff handle the security details while I ran the company. Once I stopped going on jobs myself, it was easier to stay away from humans altogether. Unfortunately, that meant I stopped visiting your father, but it was never his fault."

"Clients called you Orc? And they snapped their fingers at you?" Her piercing stare had become a stormy scowl. "What a bunch of assholes. I'm sorry you had to deal with that." She released a groan. "Fucking movie stars. They're the worst."

I stared at her, not wanting to point out the obvious.

As if sensing what was on the verge of spilling from my

lips, she threw her hands in the air. "I know, I know. I'm a mess of contradictions."

The gas nozzle clicked, and I removed it from the truck.

"At least now I know why you stopped coming around, and I'm glad it wasn't because you stopped liking us."

"That was never it."

She grinned and nodded. "Good. I guess we'd better get going then."

I twisted the gas cap back into place as Harlowe returned to her side of the truck, and I headed inside the station to pay. I should have felt relieved that she knew the truth, but with each barrier between us that fell, I felt more and more out of my depth. What would happen when there were no more walls to keep me from her?

TEN

Harlowe

"Did you get everything they had made with high-fructose corn syrup?" I eyed the snacks and sodas Roc had dumped onto the seat between us when he'd returned from paying for the gas.

He cut his eyes to the ramshackle gas station. "Does this strike you as the kind of place to offer organic snacks?"

"You're right." I choked back a laugh as I picked up a honeybun wrapped in cellophane. I hadn't eaten anything wrapped in plastic in a long time, and I found myself eagerly tearing off the wrapper.

Roc steered us from the station and out of the town, heading in the opposite direction from the farm. "The guy who owned the station said that we should stay on this road until it splits, then bear right and that will take us to the highway and to the airport."

I took a bite of the honeybun, holding it with the cellophane to avoid getting the gooey sugar all over my fingers. Now that I was away from the private jet and the strict schedule, a part of me didn't want to rush back to that life, even though it was the life I'd chosen and the one I'd worked hard to get. I made a noncommittal noise as I chewed the insanely sweet pastry and wondered why I'd ever given up sugar.

Roc swiveled his head to me for a beat as we drove down the two-lane road bordered by open fields on both sides. "Good?"

I moaned my answer then held it out. "You wanna bite?"

He started to shake his head then gave a half-shrug. "Why not?"

I twisted in my seat as I held it in front of his mouth. "I'll hold it while you take a bite. Otherwise, you'll get sticky stuff all over your fingers and the steering wheel."

I carefully guided the gooey pastry to his mouth, but just as he took a bite, the truck jolted over a bump and the honeybun smushed into his nose. I jerked it back, but not quick enough, and fake, over-processed honey covered his green nose.

I could not keep the laughter from shaking my shoulders. "I'm so sorry."

"Are you?" He was chewing as he kept his gaze on the road, but I noticed that his lips were quivering.

I pawed through our pile of snacks with one hand while I held the dented honeybun in the other. "I don't suppose we have any napkins in here?"

"No napkins."

I popped open the glove compartment, which contained a jumble of AAA maps, a small flashlight, and a lug wrench, but no napkins. I slammed it shut.

"It's fine." Roc dragged his sleeve across his nose, and I cringed as the sticky substance was smeared over his black shirt sleeve.

"Your shirt!"

"After an emergency landing, no one will expect me to look perfect." He flicked his gaze to me. "Besides, they will only be looking at you." Then he darted a look to the suit jacket folded across the seat back. "And I will put on my jacket."

I shook my head. "You are definitely not what I expected."

The sun had dipped below the horizon, suffusing the sky with gold and pink light as we drove into the sunset.

Roc flipped down his visor. "Oh? What did you expect?"

"First off, I didn't know it would be you. I suspected it would be someone from Orc, Inc., but I had no clue that you'd take the job yourself. And when I saw you, you looked so intense and serious. I remember you laughing a lot when you'd come to our house. I almost didn't know it was you."

Roc didn't respond, but he twisted his hands on the steering wheel.

"I guess we both changed over the past decade, but I'm glad to see that you aren't as scary as I first thought."

He kept his gaze locked on the road as the colorful streaks in the sky faded. "I'm sorry if I scared you."

"You were doing your job, right? A bodyguard is supposed to be scary." I covered the honeybun in the cellophane and replaced it on the seat. "I'm just glad to know that the old Roc is still in there."

He didn't respond, and I hoped I hadn't offended him as dusk fell and bathed the countryside in shadows. We continued to drive, taking the right fork in the road, without passing more than a few other vehicles. We did pass a diner with a bright neon sign followed by an old-fashioned motel with a single strip of rooms and parking spaces angled in front of them.

I eyed the sign, craning my neck to continue reading as we passed. "Did that say, 'The Velvet Cloak Inn'?"

Roc didn't have a chance to respond as the truck spluttered and coughed, jerking beneath us. He cursed as the engine rattled and spasmed, smoke oozing from under the hood and curling into the air.

"What's wrong?" I grasped the dashboard as if that might stop the violent convulsing of the truck.

"Probably a lot," Roc mumbled darkly as he steered the truck to the shoulder of the road before it gave a final shudder and died.

We sat in the cab of the truck as steam poured from under the rusty hood, the acrid smell making my nose twitch.

I glanced at Roc's tight jaw and even tighter grip on the steering wheel. "Now what?"

He exhaled, the breath hissing from him like the steam coming from the truck's engine. "We pay a visit to the Velvet Cloak Inn."

A trickle of unease slid down my spine, but I didn't know if I was more nervous about the oddly named motel or about the prospect of being stuck there with Roc.

ELEVEN

Roc

Dusk had given way to dark as we trudged along the gravel shoulder of the road, the crunch of our shoes and the rolling of Harlowe's suitcase wheels the only sounds breaking the silence of the swiftly descending night. Crickets didn't chirp, cicadas didn't sing, owls didn't hoot. Not yet, although I suspected that we'd soon be deluged by night noises.

I cleared my throat and cut a glance to Harlowe, illuminated softly by the light from her phone as she used it as a flashlight to guide her steps. She hadn't disagreed with my plan to go to the motel, but then she hadn't said anything since we'd started backtracking. I wished the woman was easier to read. I wished all women were easier to read.

I'd popped the hood of the truck to let the steam from the overheating engine spiral into the air and left it up. I'd taken the keys with me, although the locks on the doors were rusted and prone to sticking, and a hard yank would have ripped off either door. Still, I doubted anyone would steal a truck so old it appeared to be sagging into the ground one rusted hunk of metal at a time.

I would owe the farmer something for the use of his truck, although I wondered if he had any idea how close to collapse it had been when he'd watched us drive away. Did he suspect we'd end up on the side of the road or did he think the rickety truck could get us to the airfield? I was too weary to be annoyed, especially since I knew how grateful I should be that Harlowe and I were alive.

So far, I'd managed to keep her safe and out of public view, which meant I'd done my job. Maybe not in the way I'd imagined doing it, but sometimes you had to adjust on the fly.

I spotted the sign for the motel, the swirling forest-green letters lit up from below by gold light. Why anyone would choose to name a motel on a country road The Velvet Cloak Inn was a mystery. The long, squat building was painted the same dark green as the font on the sign with gold numbers on the room doors that must have once been shiny.

Harlowe sighed as we walked past the ten rooms all in a row to reach the front of the building and the reception office that boasted a glass door with a bell that jingled as we walked inside. She'd probably never stayed in a road-side motel, although something like this might be the safest place for her. No paparazzi would ever look for her here.

Even though the air was musty in the compact reception area, I detected the cloying floral scent of an air freshener that did little to hide the latent scent of cigarette smoke. A man emerged from a curtained area behind the well-worn wooden counter, swiping his hand across his forehead to smooth his comb over into place.

"Welcome to The Velvet Cloak." He smiled broadly, his eyes only flickering wider for a moment as he registered that I was an orc. He gaze paused on Harlowe, but it wasn't in recognition, only typical male interest. Good. The fewer people who recognized her, the better.

"Our truck broke down." I nodded toward the road behind us. "We need to get a tow and a couple of rooms for the night."

The man nodded. "I can call Four A Auto Repair in the next town over. They can tow your truck and get it running again." He glanced at the pegboard behind him with brass hooks for keys. "But I only have one room available."

I tracked his gaze to the singe key hanging on the board and frowned.

"But there are only a couple of cars outside." Harlowe spoke for the first time since we'd left the truck. "There's no way all your rooms are booked."

I could practically hear what she hadn't said. How could a motel in the middle of nowhere be at full capacity? Who was coming to The Velvet Cloak Inn if they hadn't been stranded on the roadside with no other option?

"They aren't booked." The man looked genuinely apologetic as he hitched up his pants with both hands. "But we had some water damage in over half of them. It was a big mess. We had to rip up the carpet and everything. What with business being slow and all, we haven't been able to finish the renovations as fast as we'd hoped." Then his expression brightened. "But you're in luck. The room we do have available is our best one. It's the honeymoon suite."

My body went rigid, and I didn't dare look at Harlowe. The Velvet Cloak Inn had a honeymoon suite?

The man cocked his head at us. "You two are married, aren't you?"

I opened my mouth to say that we weren't, but Harlowe cut me off.

"Of course, we're married." She let out a laugh that was unnaturally high-pitched as I swung my head to her in shock. "You probably wouldn't rent us the room if we weren't."

He chuckled. "I can't tell you how many teenagers we used to get trying to pass for married."

I managed to close my dangling mouth. "We're hardly teenagers."

"And I'm grateful for that." He turned and plucked the key on its plastic keychain from the pegboard. "You'll be in Room 10 down at the end. Will that be cash or credit?"

"Cash." I pulled my wallet from my back pocket and thumbed off several crisp twenties. "Will this cover it?"

The receptionist slid the bills off the counter as quickly as I'd placed them down, secreting them underneath as he nodded. "We don't have room service, but the diner next door will deliver, especially if you tell them you're in the honeymoon suite." He winked at us as he handed me the key. "Ice and sodas are right around the corner. If you need extra towels, press 0 on your room phone." He smiled broadly. "Local calls are free."

"Thanks." Harlowe spun on her heel and headed for the glass door. "Come on, honey."

I walked briskly to catch up to her as she practically stomped down the walk toward the end of the building. "Why did you—?"

She held up a hand. "Not a word until we're in the room."

I twisted to look back at the motel's reception and

found the man hanging his head out the door and watching us. He waved as if it was the most normal thing in the world. I jerked my head around with a grunt. Maybe a motel in the middle of nowhere wasn't as safe as I'd thought it would be.

When we reached room 10, Harlowe paused for me to put the key in the lock and push open the door. It swung open with a slight creak to reveal a large room with a single king-sized bed covered in a shiny red comforter and topped with a profusion of heart-shaped pillows. Over the bed and attached to the ceiling was a heart-shaped mirror.

"It's official," Harlowe said. "Hell is decorated in red satin."

TWELVE

Harlowe

I stared at the gaudy decor of the honeymoon suite. This day had gone from bad to worse to hellacious. And now I was stuck sleeping in a room where red satin came to die.

Roc stepped into the room behind me dragging my rollaboard and closed the door. "Now do you wish to tell me why you told that man we were married?"

"Isn't it obvious?" I rubbed a hand across my forehead and hoped this wouldn't give me premature wrinkles. I was too young to start Botox. "We're in the country. This isn't LA. This isn't even the 21st century if the decor is any indication. It's not the time to get hung up on honesty, especially if we want to sleep somewhere tonight."

Roc grumbled something about being able to convince the man. I glanced at his hulking form. "Maybe you're right. Maybe you could have scared the guy into giving us the room. But maybe we would have ended up with one person sleeping outside."

"I could sleep outside."

I rolled my eyes. "Just because you're my bodyguard doesn't mean you have to sacrifice yourself. I'm sure you're as wiped as I am."

He hefted my small suitcase onto the tufted stool fronting a glossy, white vanity. "I will let them know we won't make it to the airfield on time."

Roc tapped on his phone before pressing it to his ear and talking low. My phone was off, and I'd made a point not to check my messages. I knew my agent had probably left a zillion, each one reminding me how crucial the shoot was and nudging me to sign the new contract. He could stay on 'unread' until I was ready.

I barely registered Roc's words as he explained our delay, answered questions, and offered apologies. I should care that I was late to my shoot, but I was having a hard time summoning the energy to worry about something as frivolous as a movie after surviving an emergency landing.

When we'd been going down, lots of thoughts and images had flashed through my mind, but none had been about the show I starred in or the costar I'd dated. Even though our relationship had been dramatic and intense, he hadn't even merited a single thought as my brain had focused on memories with my family and even time spent with Roc.

I didn't want to think about what that meant, although I knew one thing for sure. Breaking up with Zander hadn't been a mistake. It had been the best decision I'd made since I'd started acting.

I flopped onto the bed, laying on my back and peering up as Roc wrapped up his call. The mirror on the ceiling was warped, but even so, my hair was a frizzy mess and my mascara had created dark smudges under my eyes. "Do I really look like a drunk raccoon?"

Roc set his phone on the vanity and shoved his hands into his pockets as he watched me. "I've never seen a drunk raccoon, but I'm pretty sure you don't look like one."

I pointed to the mirror. "You aren't seeing what I'm seeing."

He craned his head and tipped it to the ceiling, but I patted the bed beside me. "No way am I going to be the only one to suffer this mirror's insults. You have to lie down and look up to get the full effect." Roc hesitated, and I laughed at his severe expression. "I promise I won't bite. Besides, we're married, remember?"

He let out a guttural sound, but he lowered himself to the bed and rolled onto his back, even though he stayed as far away from me as possible while not falling off the bed. I looked up at his reflection, which only made him look bigger.

"Well, that's not fair." I swatted him. "How is it that you still look great, and I look like I've been through a tumble-dry cycle?"

"You do not look like that." He met my eyes in the mirror. "I cannot imagine that you ever look less than beautiful."

I turned my head to narrow my eyes at him. "I thought orcs had excellent vision."

He twisted his head to meet my gaze. "We do."

Heat pulsed through me as he held my gaze, and I was suddenly all too aware that we were lying on a bed of red satin beneath a heart-shaped mirror in a honeymoon suite —alone. My fingertips buzzed with the irrational urge to reach for his hand, but I forced myself to make a fist and jerk my head back to center. Even in the distorted mirror, my cheeks looked mottled and flushed.

"Despite your clear vision issues or pathological lying problem, I look like hell, and I'm starving." As soon as I mentioned hunger, my stomach rumbled as if to hammer home my point. "Should we order food and then take turns in the shower?"

Roc stood up quickly, causing the bed to jolt. "You should shower. I can go retrieve the food from the diner."

I propped myself on my elbows. "The guy at the front said they would deliver."

Roc slid his gaze to the suite's bathroom, which was connected by an arched doorway but no door. Inside I spotted a round tub as red as the satin sheets and a shower with frosted glass doors within full view of the room. Not a tremendous amount of privacy, I realized, as I swallowed hard. It wouldn't be an issue if we were a pair of newly-weds. But we weren't.

"I don't mind the walk." Roc didn't meet my eyes as he strode to the door. "You should enjoy the shower while I'm gone."

I appreciated him respecting my modesty, but the way he averted his eyes made me wonder if maybe he didn't find human women attractive. He was going way out of his way to avoid seeing me in any state of undress. I was all for chivalry, but was his reaction more than that? I was surprised to realize how disappointed I was at that idea.

Get a grip, Harlowe. He's your bodyguard, and he's a total professional, which is why he's being so discreet.

I was the one who was having all kinds of inappropriate thoughts about the orc. Thoughts I needed to rein in if we were going to be spending the night together in this not-at-all-sexy, sexed-up suite.

He opened the door and stepped out into the night, but before he pulled the door behind him, I called out his name. He hesitated, his body tensing before he glanced back at me. "It has to be this way, Harlowe."

What? I slid to the edge of the bed so my legs could hang off. What was he talking about? Did he know what I'd been thinking?

Impossible. There was no way in hell he had any idea that he'd been the subject of my fantasies for years. No way he could know that I was telling myself to keep things professional. No way he meant anything by his odd statement.

"Oookaaay," I said, "but don't you need to know what I want to eat?"

THIRTEEN

Roc

"You are an idiot," I told myself as I walked from the end of the motel with Harlowe's request for a cheeseburger—hold the mayo—and fries fresh in my mind. Of course, she wanted to give me her order. She wasn't calling me back to tell me to stay with her. She was calling me back because I was so distracted I'd almost left to get dinner without asking what she wanted.

I pulled my hair from its topknot and shook it out as I let loose a groan. What was wrong with me? I'd been off since she'd opened the door and I'd realized that she wasn't some child star. I hadn't been mentally prepared for her to be an adult or for her to be stunning. But more than stunning, she made my body react in ways I never had to a woman.

It's been too long, I thought. That's the problem.

"You've shut yourself away from the world and thrown

yourself into work, and this is what happens when you try to reenter."

I was glad no one was nearby to hear me scold myself, even though the fact that the motel was virtually deserted wasn't reassuring. Aside from a car parked near the front of the long strip of a building, there was no other sign that anyone inhabited the rooms at The Velvet Cloak. Even if most were being renovated, I doubted they ever boasted full occupancy.

As I passed the office, a quick glance told me it was empty. No reason for the attendant to stay at the desk when the chance of walk-ins was so low. Besides, he'd rented his last room to us. Thankfully, the diner wasn't as devoid of patrons.

The neon sign that flickered over the peaked-roof building with windows wrapped around three sides proclaimed that The Last Stop Diner had the world's best pie. It didn't say what kind of pie, but I suspected it didn't matter.

When I pushed through the glass door to enter, I was met by a brightly lit, clear case filled with slices of pie rotating slowly as if they were brand new models in a car show. The fluffy white toppings and lattice crusts did make my mouth water, but I wasn't there to sample pies. I breathed in the pungent scent of fried chicken and grilled meat that overpowered even the impressive display of desserts.

A waitress with a poofy blonde hairdo that looked shellacked into place leaned against a wooden hostess stand. She straightened when she saw me, her gaze roaming across my skin and then taking in my size before she tilted her head at me. "We don't get many of your kind around here."

I flinched but made sure not to show my reaction. The flat farmland we'd been driving through wasn't the kind of place that would attract orcs. Traditionally, we kept to mountainous areas. The ones of us who'd left the hills and had adapted to human society found safety in cities.

"Don't get me wrong," she continued, holding up a hand. "I don't have a problem with anyone," she eyed me, "especially not if all orcs looked like you."

"Settle down, Tracy."

I followed the voice to see a wiry man with dark skin standing in the opening to the kitchen behind the counter.

He grinned at me. "Don't mind her. Come on in and take a seat anywhere."

Tracy smiled and handed me a plastic menu then shot the cook a narrowed-eye glare.

I walked to the counter and sat on one of the few red leather stools that didn't have rips in the seat. The only other patron at the long counter was all the way on the other end, and he nodded at me before turning his attention back to his plate that looked smothered in gravy. "I'd like to order some food to go."

Tracy came around to the other side of the counter. "You want some water or coffee while you wait?"

I started to say no, but then realized I wouldn't mind a caffeine boost. I wasn't crazy about falling asleep in the motel and leaving Harlowe unguarded, but the weight of the day was already making my brain and body sluggish. "Coffee, please."

She plunked a white mug on the counter and poured a steaming stream of black coffee into it, sliding a dish of packaged creamers toward me. "You know what you want, sugar?"

I glanced at the menu long enough to confirm that they

had burgers and ordered two cheeseburgers with fries on the side.

"Good choice," the waitress scribbled my order onto her pad and thrust it toward the cook, who was already moving around his kitchen to prep my order. "Our burgers are almost as good as our pies. You sure you don't want to try a slice of our coconut cream pie?"

My stomach made a low growling sound that answered for me. I was so hungry that I could eat pie and still put away the burger with no problem, even if I shouldn't. "Why not?"

Tracy winked at me as she swished her way to the glass pie case. I took the chance to pull out my phone and read the latest texts from Harlowe's contact at the studio who arranged the second plane, which we'd missed. They were giving up on flying her to the shoot since it cost them when we'd missed the last one. They could send a car to get us, but it wouldn't arrive until the morning.

Then I scanned Jack's texts. His parental alarm came through in his series of rapid-fire questions about Harlowe, which I'd patiently answered, but he also thanked me for keeping her safe.

I knew you were the best one for the job, Roc. I knew Harlowe was safe with you.

I forced myself to shove my phone back in my pocket. My battery was dangerously low, and what else could I say? I wasn't going to tell Jack that our truck had broken down. I wasn't going to tell him that we were spending the night in a cheesy, roadside motel. I wasn't going to tell him that we'd been given the honeymoon suite with a single bed. And I absolutely wasn't going to tell him that I couldn't stop thinking about all the things I wanted to do to Harlowe in that red-satin bed.

A slice of pie topped with fluffy, whipped cream appeared in front of me, and when I glanced up, the waitress gave me another wink. "Enjoy."

I used the side of the slightly dented fork to cut the tip of the wedge, sizing up the precariously tall layer of coconut cream and whipped topping before angling it into my mouth. I closed my eyes as I swallowed, savoring the creamy sweetness. I might have been starving, but it also might have been the best pie in the world. At the very least, it was a distraction from what awaited me back in the motel room.

I might not be able to resist the temptation of sugar, but when it came to the temptation of Harlowe, I had no choice but to resist.

CHAPTER
FOURTEEN

Harlowe

As soon as Roc left for the diner, I headed for the bathroom, peeling off my clothes along the way. There was traveling grime and then there was survived-an emergency-plane-landing-and-broke-down-in-a-rusty-truck-on-the-side-of-the-road grime.

The honeymoon suite might have scored sky high on the cringe meter, but if the water in the shower was hot and the pressure was good, I was willing to overlook the mirror over the bed and the profusion of hearts.

Once I'd left a trail of discarded clothes on the tile floor and was naked, I stepped into the standing shower and adjusted the showerhead so I wouldn't get doused by frigid water. I gingerly pulled up on the nozzle and angled it to the left then flattened myself to the glass wall to avoid the water that gushed from above. I sucked in a few quick breaths, my body's response to the icy water that was splashing me even if it wasn't pouring over my head, and I waited for the warmth.

"Come on, come on." My voice cracked as I held my breath for the water to heat. A hot shower might be a small thing, but after my day, it felt like everything. If I could stand under hot, pounding water, I could wash away all the stress and panic and confusion that had whirled around me since I'd opened my front door that morning.

I held out my hand, my shoulders sagging with relief when droplets of warm water hit it. I stepped fully under the water flow, which was hot and strong, and I moaned with shameless pleasure. "Thank you, Velvet Cloak Inn."

Tipping my head back, I let the water stream over my face, down my hair, over my bare skin. I would never think another uncharitable thought about the cheesy—correction, quaint—motel. I didn't care that the decor was a throwback to the '80s, and the mirror on the ceiling was taken right out of a bad porno. None of that mattered. I was alive, and soon I would also be sparkling clean.

I swiped water from the eyes and found the body wash dispenser mounted to the wall. After pumping some of the pale-yellow gel into my palm, I lathered it over my skin and breathed in the citrus aroma. It wasn't my usual shower gel, but I'd smelled worse. I could smell like a lemon for a night.

For some reason, my mind went to Roc, who would get the second shower. The thought of him smelling like a lemon—a big green lemon—made a giggle bubble up in my throat. The guy had such a distinctive, spicy scent that it was hard to think of him being fruit-scented.

I turned under the water and twisted my neck from side to side, letting the jets pound on my knotted muscles. It had been a shock to see my dad's orc friend on my doorstep, but that moment now seemed like years ago. So much had happened between the time I'd realized that my dad had assigned my former crush to be my bodyguard and now that my head almost spun.

I'd thought that my feeling awkward was going to be the worst part of the day. I barked out a laugh. "Boy, did I call that one wrong."

It had been awkward at first, but that seemed like a faint memory when I thought about the plane malfunctioning and making an emergency landing in a field. I'd truly thought we might die, even with Roc shielding me with his large body.

Closing my eyes, I was back in the plane and engulfed by the screeching, rattling, shaking. Roc's body curled over mine had muffled some of the sound, and when I'd closed my eyes I'd been able to focus on the heat of him pulsing into me. His distinctly male scent had distracted me as I'd taken shallow breaths and finally surrendered to the possibility that I was going to die.

I shook my head hard as I pivoted and let the water hit my face, the jets sharp and stinging. But I hadn't died. I hadn't even been injured. Roc had protected me with his own body.

I almost didn't notice that I was crying until my shoulders started to tremble. I didn't know if it was reliving the accident or realizing just what a sacrifice Roc had made for me, but once the tears started, they wouldn't stop.

I didn't try to stop. I put my hands over my face and sobbed as the water poured over me, the saltiness of my tears mixing with the stream coursing down my body and swirling around my feet. I'd been pushing so hard for the past year that I hadn't had a moment to stop and feel anything. And now I was feeling everything.

I felt the barbs from social-media trolls. I felt the fear of fans who were so obsessed with me that they'd forgotten I was a person. I felt the pain from being body shamed, even though I was thin. I felt the anger that I was cast as the villain when I'd broken up with Zander, even though he'd been the asshole.

None of the people who claimed to have my best interests at heart had protected me. The show runners only cared about ratings, and my agent only cared about his cut. My costars were too busy with their own fledgling careers to think about anyone but themselves, and Zander had only ever cared about being liked more than me. My parents tried to help, but they weren't even aware of most of it. I hadn't wanted them to know.

But my dad had hired Roc. He'd known that he could trust him over all people—and he'd been right. Roc, who I hadn't seen for a decade, had taken better care of me than any of my employees or so-called friends. That made me cry even harder.

Hard enough that I didn't hear the door to the motel room swing open.

FIFTEEN

Roc

The plastic bag filled with the Styrofoam carryout containers hung in the crook of my finger as I strode down the walkway fronting the motel. The waitress had added two cans of soda to the bag and had given me a final wink after I'd handed her more than enough cash to cover the bill and a generous tip.

"Come back anytime, sugar."

Her meaning had been clear, even to someone who hadn't been around women for a long time and who had convinced himself that humans found him frightening. No one in the diner had been frightened. No one had shrunk from the sight of me. No one had made me feel unwelcome.

The truth was that my human friends had never treated me as anything but one of them. Even most of my clients had been decent, so why had I let a few bad encounters color my view so negatively? Why was it always the few horrible people who lingered in my mind longer than the kind ones? Why did an insult cling to me while I shrugged off compliments?

"It doesn't matter," I muttered to myself. I couldn't change the past. I could only move forward into a future that wasn't so isolated.

As soon as I thought about the future, my mind went to Harlowe. Although it had been years since I'd seen her and I'd only been with her for a day, I felt a deeper connection to her than I had to anyone in a long time—or ever. It made no sense that she seemed as familiar to me as an old friend and as comfortable as my own company, despite making my body jangle with a baffling torrent of emotions. She was both like slipping on a cozy sweater and being hit with jolt of electricity.

It made no sense. In my world, she made no sense. The idea of the two of us together made no sense. So why was she all I could think about?

I forced myself to push aside thoughts of Harlowe as I gave the parking area a quick scan. There were no additional cars, no people loitering outside the dingy strip building, no hints of paparazzi. One advantage to being in the middle of nowhere was that none of the reporters and photographers that usually dogged her steps had any idea where she was because no one knew where she was.

I'd been careful not to return her agent's requests for her location. After hearing her side of the phone conversation with the guy, I didn't trust him. He was too invested in Harlowe being in the spotlight to prioritize her protection. That wasn't his job. But it was mine.

But now it was more than a job to me. Protecting Harlowe was personal. She was personal. Deep in my gut, I knew that she was mine to protect, and I would kill anyone who tried to hurt her. My possessive orc tendencies had been ignited, a trait that made me a formidable bodyguard —and a dangerous one.

My fingers tingled as I remembered curling my body over hers as the plane had dropped. Despite knowing that I might die shielding her body with my own, I hadn't hesitated, and I hadn't been afraid. I'd breathed in the coconut scent of her hair and absorbed the trembles of her body, savoring the feel of her small frame being cocooned beneath my larger body. I'd protected many clients, but Harlowe was the first one I thought of as mine to protect.

But she isn't yours.

I paused in front of the door to the honeymoon suite, eyeing the tarnished, brass numbers attached to the faded, green surface. We might be sharing a single room intended for couples—lovers—but that didn't change the fact that I was working for her, and clients were untouchable.

As I shifted the plastic bag from one hand to the other and reached into my pants pocket for the room key, I detected a strange sound. I froze as I homed in on the high-pitched noise. It was coming from inside the room, and unless I was mistaken, it was coming from Harlowe.

I fumbled with the key, finally jamming it in the lock. From what I could hear through the admittedly thin wooden door, Harlowe sounded like she was in pain. Had she slipped and fallen?

Then my heart seized in my chest. Had someone found us? Was some crazed fan hurting her? All the possible reasons for her anguished sounds raced through my brain, as I dropped the bag of food outside the room and pushed the door open. Without waiting to take in the entire scene, I bolted to the source of the cries, instinct driving me to find her and stop her pain.

Fragrant steam filled the bathroom and glass shower stall, the tile amplifying the sobbing, which caused sharp talons of pain to pierce my heart. In a haze of panic, I tore open the shower door, and it came off its hinges in my hand.

Harlowe dropped her hands from her face, her wracking sobs stopping in an instant as she stood naked under the water staring at me. Her mouth dangled as her gaze went from the door in my hand to my face. Then her pained expression morphed to shocked anger. "What the hell, Roc?"

It took me a few seconds to compute what I was seeing. Harlowe wasn't hurt, she wasn't in danger, she wasn't being threatened. But she was wet and naked, and now she was mad as hell.

I opened and closed my mouth, fighting to keep my gaze on her face and not drift down to her glistening bare skin. "I heard...I thought you were..."

She flipped off the water and stomped from the shower, pushing past me to snatch a towel from the nearest rack. "I was crying, okay? It's been a long day, and we almost died." She wrapped the forest green towel around her chest as water puddled around her feet. "What the hell did you think?"

Now that she explained it, my paranoid thoughts of her being attacked seemed absurd. How could I explain that hearing her in pain had fired some deep, primal urge inside me? That wouldn't exactly make her trust me more. It would probably make her run away screaming or at the very least request another bodyguard.

She didn't wait for me to explain myself as she strode from the bathroom and left me standing with the shower door dangling from one hand and my mouth still agape. I'd never meant to invade her privacy like that or expose her, but I also knew that I would never be able to purge the sight of her perfect, high breasts tipped with pebbled, beige nipples and dripping with water from my mind.

One thought pulsed through my mind as desire pounded through my body. She was mine. But another voice whispered in the back of my brain what I also knew to be true.

Harlowe could not be mine because she was untouchable.

SIXTEEN

Harlowe

I stomped away from Roc, my damp feet sinking into the plush carpet and leaving wet footprints in my wake. Had that really happened? Had the orc body-guard who'd been my secret crush for years just ripped the door off the shower and stared at me while I was naked? There was a time when this exact scenario would have made for a very steamy mental fantasy, but the shock of it had made it more startling than arousing.

I roughly unzipped my suitcase and pawed through the contents, snatching a pair of yoga pants, clean underwear, and a T-shirt.I brusquely dried off my body before tossing the dark green towel on the bed, stepping into my black panties and yoga pants, and pulling the white T-shirt over my head. I'd moved so quickly that Roc hadn't even had a chance to emerge from the bathroom. Not that I cared.

He'd already seen me completely naked. Besides, I'd had to do partially unrobed scenes before, so I wasn't a prude. Still, I'd never had a guy walk in on me, especially not one who worked for me. I thought about my agent Grant seeing me in the buff, and a shiver went down my spine. At least Roc had seemed as shocked as I was when he ripped off the shower door.

Now that I was dressed and only slightly damp, I grabbed the towel and used it to wring out my hair. My heart had gone from thundering to beating steadily, and my anger had fizzled like a day-old soda.

I wasn't mad that Roc had seen me naked. I was upset that he'd caught me crying. I'd thought that I could let go of all my emotions in the shower where no one could hear me, but instead of it being a private release of the day's frustration and fear, Roc had seen me sobbing. I hated the idea that he'd think I was weak or, worse yet, an emotional actress who had emotional outbursts.

Then I remembered the look in the orc's eyes as he'd stood outside the shower holding the loose shower door in one hand. He'd been startled—maybe more than I'd been—but there'd been something else, something beneath the shock and embarrassment. There'd been hunger.

My stomach did a curious flip as it hit me that having a huge orc stare at me like I was something he wanted to pounce on didn't scare me like it should have. I wasn't frightened by his size or his strength or his monstrous features. I wasn't frightened by the thought of being with the orc at all. It wasn't fear that made my skin buzz and my nipples tighten. It was desire.

"I owe you an apology."

Roc's gravelly voice made me jerk, and I spun toward him, giving my hair a final squeeze with the towel and walking around him in the arch leading to the bathroom. I hung the towel on the rack, avoiding the shower door that was now propped against the wall, and returned to the bedroom. "It's fine."

He shook his head, unable to look at me. "It is not. I acted rashly and scared you. I—"

"You thought I was in trouble," I said, cutting off his apology. "You were acting out of concern for me, although the shower door doesn't thank you for it."

He kept his head down, his dark hair falling over his face and his hands in tight fists by his sides. "I violated your privacy."

"You did do that." I managed to laugh. "Listen, I know you didn't mean to burst in on me in the shower like that. If you were trying to get a peek there are more subtle ways to do it, and that was far from subtle."

He snapped his head up, the green of his cheeks dark and patchy in what must have been an orc version of a flush. "I was not trying to peek at you."

I held up my hands. "I know, I know. I was kidding."

His gaze dropped. "If you wish to have another bodyguard, I can have one of my guys replace me."

"After that show of strength and devotion? Not a chance." I made my way to the mini fridge and opened the door. "I've had a bunch of bodyguards, but none of them are as dedicated as you. Why don't we just pretend this never happened? I never cried in the shower. You never ran in and ripped off the shower door. We'll have a do-over."

"I wouldn't mind a do-over of this entire day."

I snagged a bottle of cheap chardonnay from the fridge and held it up. "I think we could both use a do-over *and* a drink."

Roc snapped his fingers and hurried to the door,

opening it, and snatching a plastic bag from the ground. "I almost forgot our food."

The sight of him pulling takeout containers from the bag made me forget everything. "You got my burger?"

"With fries and no mayo."

I moaned, as I twisted the cap off the wine and poured it into a pair of wine glasses on the vanity perched next to red napkins folded into the shape of limp swans. "You are the best."

Despite the room being the honeymoon suite, it didn't have anywhere to sit aside from the bed, so Roc stood holding two Styrofoam containers. I headed for the bed with the wine glasses, motioning with my head for him to follow me. "I guess the bed will have to be our table."

I jumped on and sat with my legs crossed as Roc sat tentatively on the edge. He placed the food on the red satin, but his back remained stiff.

I handed him a glass. "You might need this more than me."

He frowned. "I don't usually drink when I'm on duty."

I took a sip of my wine, wrinkling my nose at the sharp taste. "Then consider yourself officially off-duty. Even bodyguards get a break sometimes, right?"

He grunted, which I wasn't sure was him agreeing or disagreeing, but I was too absorbed by the savory smell of my burger as I opened the lid of my container. I lifted the top bun, grinning when I saw nothing white smeared on the inside. I tucked my wine glass between my legs to keep it from tipping over, grabbed the burger with both hands, and took a greedy bite. I closed my eyes as I chewed, thinking that it might be the best burger I'd ever eaten in my life. The wine was total crap, but the burger was greasy and thick and delicious.

I opened my eyes to say this to Roc, but I almost choked when I saw how he was watching me, his dark eyes intense as they locked on mine. Maybe I'd spoken too soon when I said he should go off-duty.

SEVENTEEN

Roc

This wasn't going to work.

I'd thought I could push aside my feelings and do my job, but all I could think about as I looked at Harlowe was seeing her standing in the shower, water droplets streaming in rivulets down her naked body. Even before I'd burst in on her showering, my mind had been distracted by thoughts of her that I'd never had with other clients. Could I protect a client who drove me to the edge of sanity and left me teetering on the precipice?

I jerked myself back from the mental cliff and dropped my gaze to my food. This had to work. I'd given Jack my word. He was my oldest human friend and the one who'd given me my start in the security business. I couldn't let him down no matter how challenging it was to be around Harlowe.

You're a professional, I reminded myself. I may not have

encountered a client who stoked my desire as much as Harlowe did, but I'd had my fair share of clients make my job a challenge. There was the porn actress who'd insisted on sunbathing naked and insisted on me standing watch over her while she did it. Then there had been a dominatrix who'd pranced around her house in little more than thigh-high boots and a black teddy. But none of them had provoked anything in me.

They didn't have the spark that Harlowe did or the girl-next-door appeal. It was because Harlowe didn't try to seduce me that made her so enticing.

I managed to shove a few crispy fries in my mouth, going through the motions of chewing while barely registering the taste. Harlowe had said she didn't want another bodyguard, but that was because she didn't understand the storm of emotions taking place within me. She didn't know how long I'd been a virtual recluse, and she didn't know how hard I was fighting the urge to touch her, hold her, taste her. And I didn't know how long I could suppress my primal instincts.

"Roc?"

Her voice seemed far away as my name drifted through the air and hung between us. I lifted my head to meet her gaze. Her brow was wrinkled, and her head angled to one side.

"Earth to Roc."

I gave my head a brief shake. "Yes?"

She laughed and mirrored my head shake. "I wanted to know if I could steal one of your fries, but I'm thinking I could have sneaked it without you noticing."

I eked out a smile as I slid my Styrofoam container closer to her. "You could have but help yourself."

She plucked a long, dangly fry from my pile and bit off

half. "I'm surprised you aren't hungrier." She motioned to her almost empty container. "I was ravenous."

"I had a piece of pie at the diner while I was waiting for our burgers."

She snagged another fry and waved it at me like a pointer. "Dessert first? I like your style."

Harlowe devoured the fry and then stood from the bed, crossed to the vanity, and poured herself more wine. How had I not noticed her drain her first glass while mine was untouched?

Maybe she was right. Maybe I did need to relax. Maybe wine was just what I needed to stop obsessing about my feelings for my client. I took a swig of the white wine and almost gasped. Maybe not *this* wine.

"Yeah, it's not great." Harlowe grinned at me as she returned to the bed and sat down with her legs crossed again. "But the more you drink, the less you notice."

I made a face at my glass. "I do not think there is enough in the bottle to make me not notice how bad it is."

"You're funny." She peered at me over the lip of her glass as she took a sip. "I don't think I remember you being funny."

Harlowe's hair draped over one shoulder, droplets of water slowly trailing onto her white T-shirt and making it even more transparent. I forced my gaze to stay locked on her eyes, the dark blue of them like deep, ocean water. "I'm surprised you remember much about me."

She rocked back and let her knees come up so she could wrap her arms around them with her wine glass still in one hand. "How could I forget my dad's best friend who was also a smoking hot orc?"

My heart thrummed and unwanted excitement danced across my skin. "You should not say that."

"Why? It's true." She drained the last of her wine in a single gulp. "You were always hot. I knew that even when I was thirteen."

I bit back a groan at the reminder that she'd been a teenager when she'd first met me. Maybe if I imagined her as the shy, gangly kid she'd been then, it would be easier to fight my attraction to her. But as I took in the actress in front of me, there were almost no traces of the kid with braces who'd avoided me.

Harlowe wasn't that kid anymore. She didn't look like her, she didn't act like her, she didn't talk like her. She was a woman in every sense of the word, and she was too much of a temptation.

"It's crazy that you haven't changed." Her teasing tone was gone as she studied my face.

I wanted to tell her that I had changed and that I wasn't the hard-bodied orc I'd once been, but another part of me didn't want to draw her attention to the fact that I was now more dad bod than hard bod. I got the sense that she didn't care about superficial Hollywood standards and wouldn't welcome body shaming, even if it was about myself.

"I know orcs don't age as quickly as humans do, but I feel like time has stood still for you while it's flown by for me." She reached out one hand and stroked a finger down my cheek. "It's like you waited for me to catch up."

My body stiffened as she scorched a seam of heat down my skin. I should stop the conversation and stop her from touching me, but I didn't do either. "Why did you need to catch up?"

Her eyes were glazed as they slid to my lips, lingering there as she nibbled her own bottom lip. "You were too old for me then, but you're not now."

My jaw was so tight I could barely grit out the words. "I am still older than you by the same number of years."

She shrugged one shoulder, the motion not much more than a twitch. "But it doesn't matter anymore. I'm in my twenties. I'm not a kid. I'm a woman. Don't you see?"

My throat was too dry to make a sound, and my body was too rigid to move, but I felt myself stumbling, slipping, falling. I did see—much more than I should.

Harlowe continued to run her finger along my face, even as I remained frozen. "I probably shouldn't tell you this, but after the day we've had, why not, right?" She leaned forward so that her lips brushed my ear. "I've always had a crush on you, Roc. A lot about me might have changed over the years, but not that."

Then she pulled back a fraction, met my gaze for a beat, threaded one hand in my hair, and pulled me into a kiss.

EIGHTEEN

Harlowe

As soon as my lips touched his, I was struck by how shockingly soft they were. Had I thought orc lips would be hard and rigid? But as soon as that thought slipped from my mind, I was struck by the startling fact that I was kissing Roc. I was kissing my bodyguard. Then I realized something else. He wasn't kissing back.

I jerked away, as if icy water had been poured over my head. What had I done? I'd thrown myself at the guy who'd been hired to protect me. Rule number one in Hollywood, don't screw—or in this case, kiss—the people you pay.

I heaved in a breath, still so close to him that I could feel his breath feathering across my lips. "I'm so sorry. I don't know what I was thinking. Clearly, kissing me is the last thing you want to—"

Before I could finish my awkward apology, his mouth was on mine. Where my kiss had been tentative, his was nothing less than a total claiming. He clasped one hand behind my head and held me to him as he opened my lips with a hard swipe of his tongue. But as forceful as his kiss was, his rough growl was followed by his tongue tangling sensually with mine.

I dropped my empty wine glass, not caring where it landed on the bed, and scraped both of my hands through his hair. In response, he swept aside the remaining takeout containers and lowered me onto my back, bracing himself over me without breaking our deep kiss. I sighed into his mouth and lifted my legs to wrap around his waist, need pounding through me and making my head swim.

As I arched into him, I felt something hard straining against his pants. Roc was so much bigger than me, than any human, that I'd always wondered how much bigger he'd be everywhere. Imagining his size had been the stuff of my teenage fantasies, and I unwound my fingers from his hair so I could fumble with the button and zipper of his pants. My fingers danced over the rigid girth that I so desperately wanted to touch, until his hand clamped over mine and stopped me.

He tore his lips from mine, his dark eyes wild and unfocused as he sucked in air. "Harlowe."

The way he said my name, it sounded like he was pleading, begging, desperate.

"Why did you stop?" I fought to even the jagged edges of my own breath. "What's wrong?"

He sat back on his knees as he raked a hand through his mane of black hair. "We can't."

I tried to laugh off his statement as I reached for the bulge between his legs. "Sure, we can. Here, I'll show you."

He grabbed my wrists on one of his enormous hands

and held them. "We should not. I am your bodyguard, and you have been drinking."

I struggled to loosen his grip. "You think I'm drunk? I'm not drunk." If I was being honest, I wasn't totally sober, either. "Is this because you think I'm too young? Too young to know how drunk I am? Too young to know when I want to fuck someone?"

He flinched at the words I instantly regretted. "I do not think you're too young. Your age has nothing to do with this, Harlowe." He pressed my wrists up over my head, so my arms were pinned above me, and he leaned over me. I couldn't have resisted him even if I wanted to, which I did not in any way. It was his turn to whisper in my ear so that his lips buzzed against the shell and sent tremors slipping down my spine. "When I fuck you, I want you to be completely sober. I want to know that you'll remember every moan and every gasp as I fill you and stretch you until you think you can't take it."

I drew in a sharp sip of air, my entire body burning as I writhed under him, wanting what he'd threatened with every traitorous cell of my being.

He nipped at my ear, his tusks scraping my flesh, but only hard enough to tease the line between pleasure and pain. "You should know, Harlowe, that when I fuck you, you will belong to me. Only me."

He released my wrists and sat back before swinging his legs off the bed. Part of me wanted to call him back and tell him that I still wanted him, that I still wanted everything he'd promised me. But I hesitated as the haze of desire started to fray at the edges.

As much as I wanted to lose myself in mind-numbing sex, I was not ready to belong to anyone. Not even to the object of my darkest and most forbidden desires. Was I?

Roc didn't look at me as he headed for the bathroom, pulling his shirt over his head and dropping it onto the floor. "I need to shower. You should get some sleep."

I was riveted to the sight of rippling muscles across his broad back and had to snatch my gaze from them when he turned and gave me a glimpse of his chest, the swell of his pecs like dark, green marble. So much for convincing myself that I didn't want him.

"You don't need to worry about me losing control again." He flicked his gaze to the carpet. "I will take the floor."

As he continued into the bathroom, I flopped back on the bed. Roc losing control wasn't even close to my biggest worry. My fear was how much I wanted him to.

CHAPTER

NINETEEN

Roc

I woke with a sharp pain in my neck as I rolled over onto the cold, hard floor and readjusted one of the heart-shaped pillows under my head. I'd barely slept, but it wasn't only the threadbare carpet that had made it difficult to sleep. It was Harlowe.

After torturing myself with an icy shower the night before, I'd returned to the bedroom to find the lights off and Harlowe buried beneath the satin covers. All my plans of apologizing for what I'd said to her had been scuttled as I stood in the dark room and listened to her rhythmic breathing. I'd had to settle for flopping onto the floor and snagging one of the many throw pillows that had fallen off the bed. But that didn't mean I'd been able to drift off. Far from it.

My night had been a series of fitful shifting, disgusted sighs, and miserable rehashing of what had happened when I'd let my primal instincts take control. I couldn't believe what I'd said to Harlowe. Worse? I was horrified that I'd meant every word of it.

When I'd been tasting her skin and breathing in the warm, feminine scent of her, I'd lost all sense of myself. I'd forgotten who I was—her bodyguard—and who she was— my protectee—and why we could never happen—too many conflicts of interest, professional boundaries, and age gaps to count. All I'd cared about was the knee-wobbling jolt I got when I touched her and how whole I felt when I held her. Every rational roadblock had fallen away like the flimsiest barrier the moment her lips brushed mine.

But now all those reasons seemed sharper than ever, especially after a night filled with regret and recriminations. My head pounded as if punishing me even further.

Suddenly, the pounding in my head wasn't the only pounding reverberating through me. Someone was banging a fist on the door.

I leapt to my feet, instantly on guard. I detected light seeping in through the thin gaps in the curtains, so I knew it was morning. Morning meant it was possible that someone from the shoot had sent a car or that somehow the paparazzi had heard about the emergency landing and tracked us down.

Glancing down at my wrinkled black shirt and pants, I closed the distance between myself and the door, peering through the peephole. I huffed out a breath of relief that there wasn't a pack of photographers angling for a shot of the starlet in the cheesy motel.

"Who is it?"

I twisted my head to see Harlowe sitting up in bed, her hair a mess and her eyes still heavy with sleep. How did she still manage to look beautiful?

"Roc?"

Her sharp tone made my back straighten as I looked through the peephole again. "Cleanshaven guy with dark, wavy hair in a fancy suit."

"Is he staring at a titanium iPhone as if it was retina-powered?"

I nodded, and Harlowe threw back the red satin covers, bustling around the room as the man outside knocked again, this time calling out, "Open up, Har. It's me."

I stepped back from the door and watched as Harlowe snatched some clothes from her suitcase and hurried into the bathroom. "It's my agent, Grant. How did he find me? Did you call him?"

"No. I only contacted the coordinator of the shoot."

I saw flashes of arms and legs in the open arch of the bathroom as Harlowe quickly changed, emerging in a clean pair of wide-legged jeans and a scoop neck, pink T-shirt. She'd swept her hair into a high ponytail and managed to look like she wasn't on the trip from hell.

She flapped a hand in the general direction of the door. "You can let him in. If he thinks I'm here, he'll never leave."

I didn't ask why she had an agent she clearly didn't love, but I did open the door.

Grant's hand was suspended in mid-knock and his mouth was open, as if he was preparing to yell through the door again. His gaze went from me to Harlowe, and his mouth didn't close.

"Hey, Grant." Harlowe cut him a brief glance as she jammed the clothes she'd slept in into the suitcase. "How'd you find me?"

Grant stepped gingerly into the room as if it might be wired to explode. "How did I find you? How did you end up here?" He slid his gaze to me and dropped his voice. "With *him*?"

Harlowe strode past her agent and shoved her carry-on bag at his chest. "Roc is my bodyguard, and he's the reason I'm alive and safe."

Grant caught the bag and hooked the straps over his shoulder as he jogged after Harlowe. "I heard about the emergency landing. I was worried sick, Har. Worried. Sick."

"Thanks." She sounded like she either didn't believe him or didn't care. She also showed not a hint of the scared, fragile woman I'd glimpsed the day before. Her voice was sharp and unyielding, and she carried herself with a confidence that bordered on arrogance.

One thing I now knew for certain. The woman could act.

"You haven't told me how you found me." Harlowe paused a few steps outside the room, and Grant almost bumped into her.

"The production assistant on the shoot." He gave her a grin that had probably charmed many a client. "When they told me they were sending a limo, I told them that I'd handle it. I wanted to see for myself that you were okay."

Harlowe eyed him carefully then glanced at the long black limousine that looked very out-of-place idling in the gravel parking lot. "How long have you been on the road?"

"Most of the night."

Her shoulders dropped an inch, and she touched Grant's arm. "You didn't have to do that. Roc took care of me."

Her agent shot me another suspicious look as I pulled her suitcase behind me and closed the motel door. "Since when do you have an orc bodyguard?"

Harlowe resumed walking once I caught up to them.

"Since my dad decided the studio's version of security was lacking." When she reached the limo, she paused. "You do remember the part where I told you he saved my life and kept me safe, right?"

Grant mumbled something that wasn't intelligible as he opened the limo door for Harlowe and cast me another tentative look before he jumped in the vehicle after her. I could now add her agent's distrust to the long list of reasons why I should stay far from Harlowe. I didn't need a slick, Hollywood hotshot looking at me like I'd crawled from the mountains on all fours.

As soon as this job was done, I would return to my isolation, and Harlowe would return to her life in the spotlight.

I would forget how sweet her hair smelled. I would forget how my skin buzzed when I touched her. I would forget how my breath hitched when I looked at her.

I would forget all of it, except for the fact that she could never be mine.

That, I would make myself remember.

TWENTY

Harlowe

" I know you don't want to talk about it—"

"Then why do I think that won't stop you?" I asked, giving my agent a side-eye glance. We'd only been riding for a few minutes when Grant had decided to break the silence of the car. Roc sat across from me with his arms crossed over his chest and his eyes closed, but I could have sworn I caught a tremor at the edge of his lips.

"You know I don't want to keep asking, Har."

"Then don't." I followed Roc's lead and closed my eyes in an attempt to shut out my agent and the questions I knew he was going to ask.

Grant released a sigh that sounded so tormented I wouldn't have been shocked if he'd revealed a hair shirt beneath his polished, cotton designer one. "It's just that the deal with the studio won't last forever. "

I didn't open my eyes. "It's been less than a day since the last time you asked."

"You know I hate to be this guy. I'm on your side, sweetie."

I wasn't always so sure about that. I had a feeling Grant was always on Grant's side. "I told you I wasn't sure about committing for another three seasons. I feel like the longer I play the bad girl, the more I'll get stuck in that role."

"A lot of actresses would kill to get famous playing the bad girl."

Everything he was saying was true. I was lucky to have the part. Lots of actresses would kill for it or kill to have steady work. Getting a three-season deal was a coup. If all of this was true, why did I get a sick feeling in my gut every time Grant mentioned it?

I finally opened one eye. "I appreciate you getting the deal for me, Grant. Truly, I do. But I need a little more time to make such a big decision. I'm sure you understand that, right?"

His cheeks mottled pink, and he patted my knee. "Sure, I do. You take all the time you need." He paused. "Actually, I don't mean that."

"I know you don't." I grinned at the guy. "Give me until the end of this shoot. After the plane going down yesterday, our truck breaking down, and us ending up in that motel, I just need some recovery time."

He nodded. "Understood." His voice lowered to a conspiratorial whisper. "You want to tell me why you were sharing the honeymoon suite with your orc bodyguard?"

"Aside from the fact that it was the only room available, and I refused to let Roc sleep on the sidewalk, nope."

His eyebrows lifted, before he made a motion of zipping

his lips and throwing away a key. "You don't have to worry about me. I won't tell a soul."

Unless you need to drum up some press, I thought, looking away from him and glancing at Roc, whose eyes were closed. There was no doubt in my mind he was listening to every word and probably had strong opinions about my agent, the deal, and my reticence to take it.

I allowed my gaze to linger on the swell of his chest muscles beneath his crossed arms, as his black shirt stretched over them and strained the buttons. As my pulse quickened, I closed my eyes to block out the sight of him.

But I didn't need to see Roc to remember what it was like to touch him. It was all too easy to be pulled back to Roc's soft lips on mine, Roc flipping me onto my back, Roc hovering over me. My fingers buzzed with the memory of moving urgently over the fabric of his pants. I'd been desperate to undress him and see all of him, feel all of him. But he'd stopped me.

Even now, I exhaled a relieved sigh. What if he hadn't stopped me? What if he'd let me unfasten his pants? What if I'd been able to finally see how large his—?

"Har?"

I opened my eyes to find both Grant and Roc looking at me.

"Are you okay, sweetie?" Grant twisted to look at me more fully. "You were moaning in your sleep."

"Was I?" I put a hand to my cheek, which was burning, and kept my gaze far away from Roc. "I guess I was having nightmares about the plane."

Grant nodded but didn't look remotely convinced. "Maybe we should have you checked by a doctor when we get to the site."

I shook my head. "I'm fine. It's just been a traumatic

twenty-four hours." That wasn't a total lie, but at this point, the part that was haunting my brain had nothing to do with the plane's emergency landing and everything to do with the hot orc sitting across from me. I could sense his gaze on me, and I shifted in place, my body sizzling with prickly heat that made it hard for me to sit still.

"But you'll be able to do the shoot?"

I rolled my eyes at Grant. "You know I would never back out." Then I put my hand on his and reminded myself that he was my agent, and it was his job to make sure I was at my best. "I promise that I'll be as good as new as soon as we get there. It will be like nothing ever happened."

I'd said the last part as much for myself and Roc as for my agent. I needed to pretend that I hadn't gotten tipsy and kissed my bodyguard, that he hadn't talked dirty to me and made me almost boneless with desire, and that I hadn't groped his cock through his pants. I needed to forget all of that if I was going to pull off this shoot and act normally around Roc.

As I turned my head away from Grant and he busied himself on his phone, I couldn't help locking eyes with Roc. He was no longer stifling his mild amusement at my conversation with Grant. His dark eyes were molten as they pinned me in place, holding my gaze to his for a moment. Then he closed his eyes and broke the spell, releasing me so I could sag into the leather seat and try to remember how to breathe.

How did I go back to normal when I wasn't the same person I'd been before he'd touched me—before he'd warned me that I would be his?

TWENTY-ONE

Roc

The wind whipped a loose strand of hair into my eyes, and I uncrossed my arms long enough to tuck it back in my messy man bun. I didn't mind the cold wind, or the fact that I was standing post outside Harlowe's trailer or that I'd rarely seen her since we arrived at the location shoot. All of that was preferable to the torture of being around her but unable to talk to her, touch her, hold her.

I let loose a low growl and squeezed my hands into fists. Harlowe had been surrounded by her agent or makeup artists or production assistants since the moment we stepped from the limo. It was as if the entire set was conspiring to keep her busy and surrounded by people.

But maybe it wasn't the people on set. Maybe it was Harlowe.

We'd never spoken about what had happened between

us. It was like we'd stepped from the motel room, and the past had been erased. The plane incident wasn't mentioned, the broken-down truck wasn't mentioned, the cheesy honeymoon suite wasn't mentioned. If I didn't remember it all in garish color, I might even believe I'd imagined it.

My gaze was unflinching as a gaggle of extras passed by, casting furtive glances at Harlowe's trailer and at me. Harlowe might not be talking, but that hadn't stopped the entire set from whispering about her near-death experience and the orc bodyguard who saved her. Their words. Not mine.

I suspected that Grant was the architect of the dramatic story, primarily because there was no mention of his starlet staying in a run-down motel in the same room as her body-guard. In the revised telling, Harlowe miraculously survived the plane crash because I shielded her, and then Grant materialized almost instantly, and whisked us all away in his stretch limousine. It wasn't a bad story, even if it did make him into a bit of a hero, and it had the advantage of not having The Velvet Cloak Inn as a backdrop.

Harlowe's agent hadn't told me not to mention anything about the motel. He didn't need to. I'd been providing security to celebrities for long enough to know that discretion was paramount. No one would ever hear a detail of my time protecting Harlowe. Not from my lips.

I stole a look at the closed trailer door and wondered if I'd get more than a brief glance and nod today. For the past two days, Harlowe had treated me exactly like a starlet is expected to treat a bodyguard. She'd pretended I wasn't there. With all the eyes on her, I understood. It was one thing to have an orc bodyguard. It was another to be involved with him.

But were we involved?

I didn't have time to debate this with myself as a wiry production assistant hurried up to me with a clipboard shoved under one arm and a pen between his teeth. He barely glanced up from his phone when he reached me. "We need Harlowe in 10, but Regina is out sick, and I have to get Tad as well, and he's going to take some cajoling." He released a long-suffering sigh. "Could you get her to set?"

I didn't know who Regina was, but I did know that Tad was the male lead and that he had a problem sleeping through his call times because he popped too many Ambiens. Harlowe might not be talking to me, but that didn't mean the hairstylists, prop masters, and gaffers didn't share gossip at craft services. Even the crafties handing out sandwiches and drinks had been sharing tales of Tad's pill-popping.

"Well?" He finally dragged his gaze from his phone and met my eyes, cowering slightly and softening his demanding tone. "Could you?"

I unfolded my arms and gave a single nod. "I'll make sure she's there. Good luck with the other one."

The PA rolled his eyes and managed a weak laugh. "Thanks. I might end up needing you to get him there, too."

He scurried off, and I turned to the trailer that I hadn't entered since we'd first been walked to it and Harlowe had allowed me to do a brief safety search before I was shown my own nearby trailer. I hesitated for a beat before walking up the steps and rapping on the door.

"Yes?" Her voice from inside was muffled.

"You're needed on set in 10," I said through the thin metal door before turning to return to my post.

The door swung open before I could descend the stairs, and Harlowe looked exasperated as she waved me inside.

She was still in her costume from the morning's scenes, which meant she was dressed in a fuzzy, Christmas sweater. "You don't have to stay out there in the cold."

I followed her inside, confused as she closed the door behind me. Did she not know I'd been standing point outside her trailer for two days? Hadn't she seen me each time she'd left and returned? "You don't want me inside with you."

She huffed at this statement but didn't deny it. "It's not about what I want. Don't you get it?"

I pivoted to stand in front of the door as she strode as far as she could get from me in the narrow trailer. "I guess I don't get it."

She threw her arms wide. "We're on a movie set with hundreds of crew and a bunch of costars who would love to knock me down a peg or two despite the fact that we're supposed to be filming a heartwarming, holiday movie. They know I just broke up with my co-star. They can't see me hooking up with my bodyguard."

"Is that what you think we would be?" An unreasonable flash of irritation pulsed through me. "A hook-up?"

She dragged her red-polished nails through her hair. "I don't know what we would be, but I do know what people would think and how people would talk. I'm sorry, Roc, but I just can't deal with any more bad publicity right now. Not on top of all the crazy threats."

My irritation faded as quickly as it had erupted. My job was to protect Harlowe, and that included from the threats, the bad press, and even from myself. "You don't need to apologize. I'm here to keep you safe. No one will hurt you, I promise."

The tension seemed to drain from her body, and she smiled at me. "Thank you. I might not have told you enough, but I am glad you're here. You're the only one I know I can trust." She practically launched herself at me, wrapping her arms around my middle and squeezing with startling strength. "Just knowing you're here makes all the crap bearable."

As surprised as I was by her embrace, I slowly curled my arms around her and allowed her to sink into me. If I wasn't careful, Harlowe switching from ignoring me to embracing me was going to give me a wicked case of whiplash. But I knew that there was no being careful when it came to her. I would gladly suffer any succulent pain she dished out and hungrily return for more.

TWENTY-TWO

Harlowe

I walked alongside the production assistant as he congratulated me on finishing the day's shoot. The sun was starting to fade, and even over the tops of the trailers, the golden glow made me smile. The location shoot was almost over, which meant I'd gotten through the experience without any negative publicity or social media scandal. I'd also managed to avoid any deranged fans and even forgot they existed for a while, which was more thanks to Roc than anything else. He'd managed all threats, and I'd been too busy to check social media. Still, it felt like closing in on the finish line of my own personal marathon.

"You're the one who deserves congratulations." I gave him a knowing look. "Tad was on his marks today."

"My secret?" The PA nudged me and laughed. "Lots of black coffee and prayer."

"For you or him?"

He nudged me again and laughed harder. "Good one." When we reached my trailer, he gave me a wave with his clipboard and peeled off, leaving me walking with Roc a step behind me.

We didn't speak as we passed crew leaving for the day. It wasn't until we'd reached my trailer and I'd walked up the attached steps and inside, that I spun around to face him. "We did it!"

The door clicked as Roc engaged the lock. "Did what?"

Some of my excitement deflated but not enough to stop me. "No one on set thinks anything happened between us. They don't have a clue. Not even Grant picked up on it, and he walked in on us in a honeymoon suite."

"I think he noticed the carpet lint on my clothes."

The reminder that Roc had slept on the shabby floor of the motel made me frown for a beat. "I guess that part wasn't a lie."

"None of it was a lie." He tilted his head at me. "Nothing happened."

Even though I was eager to sell that story, hearing Roc say it stung. "Not nothing."

"True, you did kiss me."

I huffed out a sound of pretest and put my hands on my hips. I might have been the one to make the first move, but I hadn't been the one to take it further. "So, it was all me?"

His dark eyes held mine. "I didn't say that."

I tapped one toe on the floor in rapid-fire. "I wasn't the only one who escalated things."

"Escalated?" One of his dark brows quirked. "Are we recounting a battle?"

"Maybe we are," I snapped, startled by the heat of my own words. Why was I suddenly so angry at Roc? Hadn't I been the one who'd wanted to downplay things and keep it between us? So why did it annoy me that he was down-playing what had happened between us?

"If it was a battle, then which of us won?" His voice was a low burr that rumbled into my bones.

I scrunched my lips to the side and eyed him. "You retreated."

He emitted a growl that sent a tremor dancing down my spine. "I did not retreat. I chose not to take what couldn't be freely given."

This again. I scowled at him. "Being tipsy does not mean I don't know what I'm doing." I stepped closer and jabbed a finger toward his chest. "I knew exactly what I was doing."

He didn't reply, but his eyes were pools of black as he watched me, the dark pupils swallowing all traces of color. With a tickle of unease, I wondered if I was glimpsing his primitive orc side, the side he worked so hard to hide in his expensive clothes and subdued demeanor.

I brushed away any latent nerves. I didn't care if I was provoking the monster he kept buried. I didn't care if I was releasing his primal orc side. I only cared about feeling what I had when he'd pinned my hands over my head.

I closed the remaining distance between us until our bodies were almost touching. Peering up at him, I pressed one hand lightly to his chest and felt the hard pulse of his heart through my fingertips. "I'm sober now."

Roc's jaw was so tight a muscle ticked within, and a vein throbbed. "Do you remember what I told you that night?"

My pulse quickened as I swallowed and attempted to speak in a normal voice. Instead, my words were little more than a breathy whisper. "You told me that I will belong to you."

He hadn't moved his arms as he loomed over me. "When will you belong to me, Harlowe?"

My breaths were so shallow that I felt dizzy staring up at him, but I also couldn't tear my gaze from him. He was going to make me say it. Make me be the one to escalate.

I hesitated, before realizing I didn't want to retreat. I didn't want to run from this or from him. "When you fuck me."

He nodded so softly the movement barely registered. "That was your first warning. This is your second."

Then his mouth was on me with such ferocity that I didn't take a breath or open my eyes until he'd backed me to the table and was lifting me onto it. The only coherent thought in my mind was that I desperately wanted his third warning.

TWENTY-THREE

Roc

I took long steps across the compact trailer, backing Harlowe with me until I could hoist her onto the table so that her legs fell open, and I could stand between them. When I tore my lips from hers, she peered at me, her pupils flared dark, and her lips swollen plump.

My heartbeat quickened as my hands traced the curves of her body and I leaned in to capture the hollow of her throat with my lips, nipping my way to the spot behind her ear where her pulse thrummed. "Tell me that you're mine."

I hungered to hear her breathy words of submission and to know that one who was not easily possessed wanted me to take her.

"Maybe *you're* mine." Her eyes glinted with challenge as she hooked her legs around my waist.

I inhaled the warmth of her neck and tasted the faint sweetness of her skin on my tongue. Her pulse fluttered as I growled and tugged my pants down roughly with one hand. "You believe yourself to be in a position to argue?"

She raked her hands through my hair, the nails scoring my scalp and provoking a hiss as I savored the dance between pleasure and pain. She jerked back my head so that our gazes met. "Control is relative."

My head swam with the desire to plunge myself into her, and I ran the tips of my tusks along the delicate flesh of her throat. "You think you are in control?"

She heaved in a breath and rocked her hips forward, grinding herself into the hard bar of my cock. "What do you think?"

I huffed out an impatient breath, gritting my teeth so hard I heard the sound over the hum and buzz of the trailer's generator. This female was nothing like other starlets I'd protected. But I'd never wanted any of them. It was only her pledge, her promise, her prize I wanted.

I cupped her face in one hand, watching her wide eyes as I dragged my free hand to the small of her back and jerked her flush to me. "I think you want to give me what I want."

"And what do you want?"

I rasped my thumb across her full bottom lip. "I want you to tell me that you belong to me. I want to hear my name on your lips as I fill you."

She bit back a moan when I reached beneath her flared skirt and nudged her lace panties to one side. I bent down, keeping my gaze on her as I slid her skirt up. Then I buried my face between her legs, sliding my tongue inside her and savoring the slick, honeyed juices.

Harlowe gripped my shoulders, her nails digging into my skin through my shirt as I lapped at her, my tongue flicking over her clit almost languidly. I was enjoying the taste of her almost as much as I was relishing the fervent twitching of her hips and soft keening sounds that escaped her lips. When I slipped one finger inside her, moving it deftly and slowly, Harlowe bucked up, her legs quivering and her body spasming on my tongue and around my finger until she went boneless and released her grip on my shoulders.

Standing, I licked my lips, a primal growl vibrating in my chest. I grabbed the sides of her panties and tore them off her, watching the black lace flutter to the floor. Without uttering another word, I freed my cock, fisting the base of it and sliding it to her wet entrance.

Harlowe was propped on her elbows as she sucked in air. "Not fair."

I pushed just the crown of my cock inside her and watched her blue eyes flicker with need. "No? Should I stop?"

She bit the corner of her lip. "Don't stop. Please."

My own grip on control was tenuous, but I restrained myself from thrusting wildly into her. "Please what?"

Her eyes rolled back in her head. "Don't stop. I need you inside me."

I bit down on my own lip to keep from exploding, and I tasted the metallic tang of my own blood. "Tell me what you want, Harlowe."

She moved her hips restlessly, as if straining for more, but her breath was uneven, and her chest heaved.

I bent over, bowing my head so that my lips crowded her ear, my words furtive and low. "Do you want me to fuck you?"

She bobbed her head up and down, but my voice was husky in the darkness. "Say it."

A sigh escaped from her parted lips. "I want you to fuck me, Roc."

A satisfied sound rumbled from my throat as I thrust into her in a single hard motion and relished the gasp of her pleasure. Harlowe threaded her hands through my hair and yanked my head down, pulling my mouth to hers. I continued to move inside her as our tongues tangled, the sensations storming through me hot and fierce.

Her body was tight and hot, gripping my cock like nothing I'd ever experienced before. It was all I could do to keep from detonating as she met each thrust greedily, her desperate cries swallowed by my mouth. When her body began to tighten around my cock, I tore my lips from hers as I reared back and roared with my pounding release, the noise echoing through the trailer.

Then I fell forward, holding her sagging legs as they slipped down from my waist and burying my head in her neck as we both fought for breath.

"So much for keeping things quiet," Harlowe said with a throaty laugh. "They might have heard that back in Beverly Hills."

At that moment, I didn't care if they did.

TWENTY-FOUR

Harlowe

I rolled over, bumping into something hard. I groggily opened my eyes, expecting to see a bolster pillow, but what I was staring at was huge and olive green. I sat up, instantly awake.

Roc. I was in bed with Roc.

Then I remembered why I'd collapsed into bed with my bodyguard the night before and my cheeks burned. My gaze lingered on his bare chest scattered with dark hair, but I'd seen much more than his sculpted muscles while we'd been going for round two up against the cabinets and round three in bed.

I rubbed my forehead. *Harlowe, Harlowe, Harlowe. What have you done?*

I'd jumped from one publicity disaster and right into a potentially even bigger one. Fans already weren't happy that Zander and I had broken up and considered me the villain, but what would they say if they thought I'd cheated on him with my orc bodyguard? It wouldn't even matter that it wasn't true or that I hadn't even laid eyes on Roc when I'd ended things with Zander. People would spin it as me being the bad girl and Zander being wronged. For some reason, fans loved that handsome prick.

"Because they have no idea what a dick he is," I mumbled, as dark thoughts of my manipulative ex filled my head.

"I hope you aren't talking about me."

I jumped and put a hand to my chest. I'd been so distracted by my own thoughts, I hadn't noticed that Roc had opened his eyes.

"Of course not." I laughed it off, as I self-consciously wrapped the yellow sheet around my chest and swung my feet off the bed, almost banging my toes into the wall. The sleeping area in the back of the trailer was snug, but even more so with a massive orc taking up more than half the bed.

I'd had no regrets last night, especially not when I was coming for the third time, but in the bright light of day I wasn't so sure about my impetuous decision. Most of my career had been defined by careful decisions, not wild nights that made my cheeks flush when I thought about it.

Roc hadn't seemed like a mistake when I was straddling him in bed. Then again, the best mistakes never felt that way in the moment.

I stood, tugging the sheet with me. When I glanced over my shoulder, I saw that I'd taken all the fabric with me, leaving the orc completely exposed. My face burned even hotter as my gaze locked on his dark-green cock that was impressive even when it wasn't rock hard. "Crap, I'm sorry."

"I should get up anyway." He stood without any trace of embarrassment and padded barefoot across the trailer, plucking his clothes from the floor as he went. My mouth became as dry as Palm Springs as I watched his perfect ass and his long, muscular legs. When I got a glimpse of his cock swinging between his legs from behind, I forced myself to stop staring.

"I'm glad I only have a few more scenes to shoot." My voice sounded artificially bright to my ears, but anything was better than silence and me gaping at him like a creeper.

Roc pulled on black boxer briefs and turned to face me. "You're eager to get home?"

"It's always nice to get back to normal life." I traded my sheet for a white, terrycloth robe hanging on a hook near the bed and slipped into it without rushing too much or appearing to be some kind of sex kitten turned nun. "Won't you be glad to get back to your own place?"

His eyes didn't dart from mine as he watched me tie my robe closed. "I won't lie and say that I'll miss these trailers."

I laughed. The trailers might be considered luxurious, but they were still houses on wheels. "This is my first trailer with a bed. The one for the show has a decent couch but I never have to sleep there, so…" I let my words drift off when I realized that I was babbling.

"Sometimes beds come in handy."

The husk of Roc's voice sent an arrow of heat through me, and for a moment I considered throwing myself at him again. His lips were curled up at the edges and his meaning was clear. If I dropped my robe, he wouldn't object for even a heartbeat.

Our gazes held as we stared at each other across the length of the trailer. Should we talk about what happened? Was it necessary to say that it had been a one-time thing, or did he know that? He might have said that I was his, but I was pretty sure that was just sex talk, right?

I was the first to look away, as I cleared my throat. "I should probably get ready for the last scenes."

Roc stepped into his black pants, which were wrinkled from their night on the floor, and then shrugged on his shirt, tucking it into his pants without responding to me.

I was riveted to watching him dress, the process of him buttoning his shirt mesmerizing me as if he was performing magic. He caught me watching him, and his fingers stilled. "Harlowe, I—"

I held my breath in wait for what he was going to say, but a sharp rap on the trailer door cut him off. I almost stamped my foot with impatience as I stepped to the door and opened it a crack, preparing to tell whichever production assistant had interrupted us that I needed more time. But it wasn't a production assistant.

Cold chills went through me, as if I'd been doused with freezing water, as I tried to process who was outside my trailer.

"Surprise, babe!"

TWENTY-FIVE

Roc

"Zander?" Harlowe's voice warbled, and her knuckles went white as she clutched the doorframe. "What are you...?"

Zander. Her costar and recent ex-boyfriend.

"Aren't you going to let me in, Har?"

She didn't step back to open the door wider. "I'm shooting soon. You should have told me you were coming."

"If I told you, it wouldn't be much of a surprise, would it?" He laughed, as if his unannounced arrival had surprised and delighted even him.

"This is my last day of shooting. Maybe we can talk afterward."

"Seriously?" The levity had dropped from his voice like a cheap costume that came in a plastic pouch. "You aren't going to let me in? I just want to talk, babe. You owe me that."

The hackles on the back of my neck prickled. How many men had I heard tell women exactly what was owed to them, usually before demanding more than they deserved?

I stepped forward to intervene, but Harlowe was already backing up as a tall twenty-something with spiky hair and cold blue eyes pushed his way past her and straight into me.

"Whoa." He almost bounced off my chest, thrusting his hands up to push himself away from me. "Who the fu—?"

"I'm her bodyguard, and you don't seem to understand when a woman is saying no."

Harlowe backed away, holding her robe closed with one hand, her gaze bouncing between the two of us. The actor might have been tall, but I was taller. I also had muscle and tusks, while he was slim and had perfectly bleached teeth.

It took Zander about a breath to assess me and realize he was on the losing end of the pissing contest. He held up his hands. "My bad." Then he cut his gaze to Harlowe. "I didn't know you had a bodyguard staying with you."

"He's not staying with me," she said much too quickly as she avoided my gaze and narrowed her eyes at him. "After we broke up, I got a lot of bad press and some crazies threatening me online, or did you not know that making me look like the villain in our breakup would incite a troll mob?"

Her rushed denial that I wasn't staying with her had not been what I'd been expecting, but I reminded myself that it was the truth and that actors in Hollywood talked. From what I'd heard, this one talked too much.

He flashed a smile he probably thought was charming, but it faded when she didn't return it. "I had nothing to do with that, babe. You know what it's like with publicists."

My gaze hadn't left Zander, and it bored into him now.

How had Harlowe been involved with such a coward? He was clearly used to getting his way and getting away with all his bad behavior. I curled my hands into fists, inhaling and exhaling steadily to keep myself from removing him from the premises by force.

He flicked a nervous glance at me and then away just as quickly. "Can we talk privately, Har?"

Harlowe shook her head. "Like I said, this isn't a good time. I have to be on-set soon."

He took a small step toward her, cocking his head like he was trying to calm an agitated dog. "Don't be like this, babe. I came all this way because we were good together, and we can be that way again."

"You want to get back together?"

"We may have fought a lot, but I never stopped loving you, babe."

Harlowe made a strange, high-pitched sound in her throat. "We were miserable together."

His apologetic expression twisted for a beat. "I've learned a lot since we broke up."

"It was only a few weeks ago. How much could you have learned in a few weeks? You barely learned your lines on time."

Zander flinched at this, but his grin rallied. "I came here to win you back, Har. We belong together. You know it. I know it. We were magic together, babe."

Every molecule in my body wanted to pummel this arrogant asshole. What I wanted even more was for him to know that he'd been replaced. Harlowe wouldn't be getting back together with him or getting together with anyone else because she was with me. She was mine.

I allowed my gaze to leave Zander and go to her, fully expecting her to be vibrating with the same anger that pulsed through me. But she wasn't. She gnawed at her lower lip while shifting from one foot to the other.

"I don't know," she finally said, the words rushing from her mouth. "All I know is that I can't do this now. I need to change."

Zander's smile was one of triumph, but I felt like I'd been sucker-punched. She didn't know? I cleared my throat, giving myself a second to get my emotions under control. "Harlowe—"

"I need to focus on my scenes." The words that cut me off were as sharp and cool as shards of ice. "That means I need everyone out."

I managed to steer the punk actor from the trailer as I left without a backward glance. I paused on the top step after pulling the door shut behind me.

"Don't take it personal, man." Zander pivoted when he reached the ground. "She hasn't changed all that much in a few weeks either, and she's never liked bodyguards."

I grunted, thinking that it was very personal, but he also might be right. Some things would never change—including me.

I'd known at my core that getting involved with a client was a mistake. As I walked away from Harlowe, I couldn't blame her from proving me right. The mistake had been mine, but it was one I could undo.

TWENTY-SIX

Harlowe

I blew into my hands to warm them the moment the director called cut, my shoulders sinking with relief. That was it. I was done with my scenes. I could go home. I could get back to my normal life. I could unravel my current mess.

With a grin and a wave, I headed for my trailer, both anticipating and dreading the apology I owed Roc. I'd been in a state of confusion and shock when I'd dismissed him, but it hadn't been his fault that Zander had shown up unannounced. He hadn't deserved me taking out my stress on him.

And then there was Zander. What did he deserve? A kick in the balls? A second chance? Something in the middle?

My gut told me that getting back together with him was a mistake. "Especially since you spent last night getting your brains fucked out by someone else," I muttered under my breath.

My face heated at the memory of just how up close and personal I'd gotten with my bodyguard. And during all of it, I hadn't thought about missing Zander once. I hadn't regretted it. I hadn't wished it was him in bed with me instead of Roc. I hadn't felt an ounce of embarrassment— until my ex had shown up. Then the reality of having fallen into bed with the guy sworn to protect me had seemed all wrong.

That still didn't mean I wanted to get back together with the jerk who'd made my life hell. So why had I hedged when Zander had suggested it? Why hadn't I told him to shove his stupid idea right up his...?

"There you are, babe."

I jumped as Zander sidled up next to me and draped an arm around my shoulders. "You have got to stop sneaking up on me."

He didn't withdraw his arm, but he did make a tsk-ing sound in his throat. "So touchy."

"Sorry, I've been shooting all day." Wait, why was I apologizing to him?

"I know. I've been waiting for you. By the way, the coffee cart here is great. They made me a perfect oat milk vanilla latte."

"Great."

"You want me to get you one?"

So, he hadn't picked up on my dripping sarcasm. And he didn't remember that I despised oat milk. I spun out from under his arm so that I was facing him. "Listen, I know you traveled all the way here to talk, but I need to take care of a few things first."

"You finished your scenes." He eyed me with genuine

confusion. "What else could be more important than talking to the boyfriend who flew here to see you?"

"Ex-boyfriend," I corrected. "And I need to apologize to Ro—my bodyguard. Then we can talk."

Zander opened his mouth, but Grant rushed up before he could speak. "There's my favorite 'it' couple!"

I frowned at my agent. "We're not a couple anymore, Grant." Was I the only person who remembered our messy breakup that had then played out over social media and made it necessary for me to need a bodyguard?

Grant glanced at Zander then at me. "I know you two have had your ups and downs, but the world loves Harlowe and Zander together. I loved Harlowe and Zander together. The studio loves Harlowe and Zander together."

"See?" Zander beamed at me. "Everyone knows we should be together. It's a win-win-win."

There was something in the brief glance between Zander and Grant that made my senses tingle. "Does this have anything to do with the contract negotiation?"

Grant's mouth fell open, and he pressed a hand to his chest. "What?"

"Come on, Har." Zander grabbed my hands. "You have to know that both of our value to the studio goes up if we're still the golden couple of their series."

Grant's head bowed, and he released a breath as if defeated.

I snatched back my hands. "This was all about money? You came here to get back together so you could get more money?"

"We'd both get more money, babe." Zander smiled at me like he hadn't just admitted betraying me—again. "And I do want to get back together. I miss waking up with you, Har."

So, he was greedy and horny. At least he was staying on brand.

I backed away from both men, so disgusted I was afraid I might throw up on them. Not that they didn't deserve it.

Tears burned the back of my eyes and blurred my vision as I stumbled forward. I needed to get out of here. I needed to get far away from my agent and my ex and every guy who'd broken my trust. Then I stopped and swung my head around, searching for the big, green figure who'd been my constant shadow for the past few days. I needed Roc.

I ran the rest of the way to my trailer, racing up the steps and bursting inside. "Roc?"

Only my voice echoed back to me in the empty space. He wasn't there. I ran back outside and down the stairs, my gaze sweeping the area.

"Has anyone seen my bodyguard?" My voice was shrill, but I didn't care. Let them call me bitchy and demanding. I needed the one guy who'd shown me that he would protect me.

A PA I recognized stopped as he was hurrying past. "Tall, hot, and green?"

I nodded. "Do you know where he is?"

"He left."

The new voice was deep and gravelly, and I swiveled to see another orc dressed all in black standing with his hands clasped in front of him. "I'm your new bodyguard, Cort."

TWENTY-SEVEN

Roc

"You're sure about this?" I asked as I climbed the stairs into the studio's private plane with Mason leading the way.

The production assistant bobbed his head up and down without glancing back, looking just as in charge as always, even without his trademark clipboard. "I'm sure. No one needs it until tomorrow, and I told my boss that Harlowe's team needed it. After the disaster of getting you all here, he was fine with it. Besides, you need to get away fast. I get that."

I paused at the top of the steel stairs as he hesitated in the open door of the plane. "I'm not leaving my client without protection."

"Oh, I know. Who do you think met your colleague on the tarmac earlier?"

I shifted from one foot to the other. "Thank you for helping me arrange the staff change."

Mason's brows peaked. "Is that what we're calling it?" Before I could repeat the canned line about needing to return to my office and have one of my orc bodyguards take over the job of getting Harlowe safely home, he fluttered a hand in the air. "Don't worry. I don't like seeing her with him either."

"This isn't about Zander." Even saying the name out loud made my upper lip curl.

His brows hadn't lowered but he patted my arm roughly. "I know how hard it is to see clients make dumb mistakes, especially when they've made them before. I work in the film industry, remember?"

I breathed out, on one hand relieved that he thought I was leaving because I didn't want to see Harlowe repeat her bad relationship with her co-star but also insulted that he thought I would so easily leave an assignment. I'd never abandoned one before and I wouldn't be leaving now if it didn't feel like being punched in the kidneys every time I had to watch Zander touch her.

What had been most painful had been the fact that she hadn't told him to get lost. She hadn't told him that she couldn't get back together with him because she was involved with someone new, and she hadn't treated me like anything more than her bodyguard when she'd sent me away.

I guessed I should be glad that Mason didn't know there was anything between me and my protectee. I managed a gruff nod. "Harlowe's mistakes aren't my business."

Not anymore, I thought.

Mason stepped back to allow me inside the plane,

sweeping his arm at the interior with a flourish. "Thanks again for helping me get her to set on time this week. I'll definitely recommend you to my clients."

I didn't tell him that this was the last job I'd be doing personally. Coming out of my semi-retirement had proven to me that I was better off working in the background managing my team of orc bodyguards.

Instead, I held out my hand. "My company is at your service."

He took it, his fingers vanishing into my much larger palm. "Have a safe flight, Roc."

He released my hand and jogged back down the stairs to the tarmac while I stepped into the luxurious jet where everything was cocooned in buttery beige leather and warm woodgrain polished to a high shine. I glanced around as if expecting someone to leap out and say that I was in the wrong place.

It wasn't that I was unaccustomed to traveling in style. I'd flown with enough wealthy clients to be accustomed to their jets. But I'd never flown in a private plane without being someone's staff. I'd always been on duty, on alert, on the job.

I picked one of the wide seats and sank into it, glancing out the window where the sun was setting and sending golden shards of light splintering across the sky. As pretty as it was, I flicked the shade down. After the emergency landing on my way to the shoot, I preferred to pretend what I wasn't hurtling through the sky to get home.

I rested my head on the back of the seat and closed my eyes, allowing my body to focus on the vibrations from the engines and the clattering sounds outside the jet as they prepared for us to leave. Even as my heart was a twisted ball of suppressed pain, it was beginning to soften now that

I knew I was leaving. I was returning to my safe haven, my refuge, my home.

There would be fallout from my departure, but I was willing to deal with that. I could offer my apologies to Jack along with the evidence that I'd protected Harlowe until the end of the shoot. Until I couldn't any longer.

I despised the idea of keeping the truth from my friend, but the truth wasn't mine to tell. Most importantly, it didn't matter anymore. Harlowe had made her choice, and it hadn't been me.

I squeezed my eyes together, desperate to purge my mind of the memories of being with her. Even more than ridding myself of that torment, I wished I could banish the memory of her sending me away like the hired help I was to her.

"In time," I whispered to myself like a mantra. In time, I would forget the pain of this rejection, just like all the other rejections and slights in my past had faded.

"What in the actual fuck are you doing?"

My eyes flew open, and I had to blink a few times to register the woman standing in the aisle with her hands on her hips and her eyes blazing.

"Harlowe?"

CHAPTER
TWENTY-EIGHT

Harlowe

By the time I reached the top step of the glossy white jet, the steel staircase rattling under the onslaught of my stomping, I was both seething with rage and sucking in breath. Did he really think he could ghost me? Did he think he could substitute another orc bodyguard in his place, and I wouldn't care? Did he think he could walk away without a word of explanation?

I'd had the entire drive to the private airstrip to think of what I was going to say to Roc if I was able to catch his plane, but I'd been vibrating with too much betrayal and anger to come up with much more than screechy accusations. Luckily, the PA who'd agreed to drive me in her battered Toyota hadn't asked any questions when I'd told her I needed to stop Roc from leaving. Only Zander had been thoroughly confused when I'd raced past him on the way to the car, ignoring his pathetic pleas for me to let him explain.

I'd ignored him. His explanations were nothing more than more empty lies and meaningless promises. I was done with liars and cheats. I was done with Zander. And apparently, I was also done with my agent since I'd told Grant that he could shove his studio deal and our contract up his ass.

If I hadn't been so furious with Roc, I would have savored the shocked look on Zander's face and the way Grant's jaw had hit the floor. But I couldn't think about either of them or the fallout from my knee-jerk decisions. The only thing filling my mind was the fact that Roc had been the only one I could trust, and he'd left me.

I burst into the small plane's cabin, heaving in air as I glared at the orc sitting peacefully in a window seat with his eyes closed. Instead of the sight of him calming me, it made me even more livid that he appeared so unaffected by ditching me.

"What in the actual fuck are you doing?"

He opened his eyes, staring at me for a few beats as if he didn't recognize me. "Harlowe?"

"What?" I rapped my foot on the plush carpet, which muffled any sound. "You already forgot who I am? You really did move on fast."

He stood slowly, the olive-green skin of his brow furrowing. "Move on? You are accusing me of moving on?"

I flinched at the accusation implied in his words. "You're the one running."

"I'm not running. I'm leaving after completing an assignment."

My pulse tripped as rage pulse through me. "An assignment? Is that all I am to you? A job?"

130

"I never said that." He took a step closer. "You are the one who sent me away. You are the one who pretended I was nothing more than your employee as soon as your ex-boyfriend appeared."

The backs of my eyes burned at the sting of truth. I had reacted badly when Zander had surprised me, and I hadn't been brave enough to admit that Roc was more to me than a bodyguard. How would I have felt if he'd done the same thing to me? Would I have stuck around to see if I was pushed even further to the side?

Suddenly, my fury at him morphed into anger at myself. I wasn't mad at Roc. I was mad at myself for not being brave, for not saying what I wanted, for not standing up for myself and for him. My body sagged as if the only thing that had been keeping me upright had been my misplaced rage.

I stumbled to the nearest seat and slumped into it. "You're right. I was a coward."

Roc didn't say anything for a moment then he knelt in front of me. "I understand being scared."

A laugh of disbelief bubbled up and spilled from my lips as I looked up and met his gaze. "Scared? When have you ever been scared? You're big and brave and tougher than anyone I know."

His lips curled into a sad smile. "You scare me."

I narrowed my eyes at him, not sure if I'd heard him right. "How can I scare you? I'm not that demanding of a client, am I?"

"No." He reached for my hands. "But you make me feel things I've pushed deep inside for a long time. I'd convinced myself that being alone and protecting my heart was playing it safe, but when I'm with you I can't play it safe. You scare me, Harlowe, because you make it impossible for me to keep my heart safe. You make it impossible for me not to feel."

I watched his mouth moving, but I couldn't quite comprehend what he was saying. "You feel...what?"

He drew in a long breath. "I love you, Harlowe. I know I shouldn't. I know we shouldn't, but I think I've loved you since you opened your door that first day."

A part of me had thought that what had happened between us had just been heat that needed to be burned off, but a deeper part of me also knew that I'd been drawn to him since I'd seen him standing on my doorstep. He might have started out as a childish crush, but what I felt for him now was something much deeper. It was fast and crazy, but I knew in my gut it was real. "I love you too, Roc, and I'm so sorry if I ever made you feel like I didn't."

I launched myself into his arms, almost knocking him off his feet. He managed to stand up as I clung to him and wrapped my legs around his waist, holding on as if he might run away again if I released my grip.

"What now?" he whispered into my ear.

"Well, I told Zander to fuck off, and I fired my agent, so I guess I'm leaving with you."

He squeezed me. "And when we get back to LA?"

I pulled back so that I could meet his uncertain gaze. "I guess we become the hot gossip for fifteen minutes before people get bored. Then we see what normal life looks like for us."

"Sounds perfect," he husked before threading a hand through my hair and pulling my mouth to his for a kiss that made me forget every bad thing that happened before it. As he deepened the kiss and unleashed a deep growl, I forgot everything else entirely.

TWENTY-NINE

Roc

I let my hand hover over the door, hesitating before I knocked. I hadn't seen Jack since I'd returned from the shoot with Harlowe or since she'd told him that we were involved. I'd wanted us to tell him together, but she said she couldn't keep anything so important from her parents, and she didn't want them to read about us in the tabloids first.

So far, the tabloids hadn't latched onto the juicy gossip of a rising starlet dating her orc bodyguard but only because we'd managed to stay out of sight, but that wouldn't last forever. As much as I wanted to keep our relationship a secret, Harlowe insisted that she didn't want to hide me. Step one in that was telling her family. Step two was me joining them for dinner.

I gulped as I lingered on the threshold of the house. I hadn't been this nervous since I'd stood on Harlowe's doorstep, startled that the girl opening the door wasn't a girl anymore.

Finally, I rapped on the wood and stepped back, jumping when the door was flung open. Jack stood on the other side, just as tall as I remembered but with gray in the temples of his short, brown hair. Despite looming over him, my heart hammered in my chest. I might be bigger and stronger, but he possessed something I desperately wanted —approval.

"Jack," I managed to croak, my voice unsteady.

The man eyed me seriously for a moment before his face broke into a smile. "Come on in, Roc. It's been too long."

The breath whooshed from my chest as I entered the house, my nerves still jangling. He looked just like the Jack I'd known for years. Just as friendly. Just as welcoming. Maybe Harlowe hadn't told him after all.

He thumped a hand on my back as he led me through the foyer and into the open living room. Jazz was playing in the background, and the air held the distinctive aroma of grilling burgers. "I'm glad you could join us. Can I get you a beer?"

Okay, she definitely didn't tell him. I paused before he could lead me to the sliding glass door that opened onto the back patio and the grill area. "Jack, I think you should know—"

"Harlowe told me." He gave my back a harder thwack. "I'm not going to say I wasn't surprised, but she assured me that she was the one who pursued you. Chased you down, is the way she put it."

My face warmed. It would be a lie to say that I wasn't a fully invested participant in everything that had happened between us. "Our feelings are mutual."

Jack smiled. "I'm sure they are." He shook his head. "Not that I need to know anything more about it."

I put a hand on my friend's arm. "I want you to know that I never allowed my feelings to affect my work in protecting her. I would never allow Harlowe to be hurt, and I would never hurt her."

Jack held my gaze as an understanding passed between us. "I know. Like I said when I called you, there isn't anyone I trust more than you to protect my daughter."

The glass door slid open and Harlowe rushed in with a happy yelp as she jumped into my arms. I took a step back as she curled her legs around my waist and kissed me hard. So much for easing her family into the idea of the two of us together.

It was hard to remember my plan of restraining myself around her family when Harlowe's lips were pressed against mine. When she pulled back and grinned, sliding down my body until her feet hit the floor, she grabbed my hand and tugged me forward. "Come say hi to the rest of the family before my dad decides to steal you for himself."

I shot Jack an apologetic look as I followed his daughter, but he just shook his head. "Now you understand what I deal with."

Harlowe's mother gave me a hug as we walked onto the back patio, and her two little sisters ran up and wrapped their arms around my legs, begging me to walk around with them. Despite Harlowe telling them to stop pestering me, I was happy to walk around the back yard with the two girls clinging to my calves like sloths and giggling until they fell off and rolled around in the grass.

"Jack is thrilled you're here, Roc," Harlowe's mother told me once her younger daughters had run off to play on the wooden swing set. "You can help him balance out all the girl energy."

"If anyone can, it's Roc." Jack had taken up his post at the grill and now wore a red-and-white striped apron over his jeans and green Henley.

"I'm happy to be here." Despite my initial nervousness, I was glad to be with Harlowe's family. It had been many years since I'd spent time with them, but it felt like no time at all, as I slipped back into the comfortable and familiar routine of talking with Jack while his wife sipped wine and let him grill dinner.

The only differences were that now Harlowe shared a glass of wine with her mother as they stretched out on lounge chairs on the flagstone patio, watching the younger girls playing. Jack handed me a beer as I stood next to him at the grill, the savory aroma of burger meat making my stomach growl as we talked business.

When Harlowe joined me, linking her fingers in mine as her dad carried the tray of cooked burger patties to the table, she squeezed my hand. "How does it feel to be back?"

My throat was tight as I peered at her. "I feel like part of the family again."

"You were always part of it." She leaned into me and rested her head on my chest. "You just forgot."

I kissed the top of her head as warmth spread through me. "Thank you for reminding me."

Harlowe tipped her head back, giving me a wicked smile. "The pleasure is all mine."

A growl hummed in the back of my throat. "I assure you it isn't."

"Maybe not." She lowered her voice. "But that sounds like something we should settle later when we're back at my place."

"Or mine."

She squeezed my hand again. "I love having you here again. It feels so right. *You* feel so right."

I knew exactly what she meant. Being together had always been our destiny. It had just taken us a while to find each other again. "I love being here with you and your family. I love *you*."

Her pupils flared. "Oh yeah? Well, I love you more."

Impossible, I thought as my heart squeezed so hard it ached. "I should warn you, now that we've found each other again, I have no intention of ever letting you go."

"Good. I'd hate to have to chase you down again."

"Food's ready!" Jack called from the table.

As Harlowe turned to join her family, I pulled her back and whispered in her ear. "I'll always let you catch me."

"Well, you can try to catch me," she teased as she scooted away from me. "But I make no promises."

"Game on," I laughed as I followed the woman I adored. "Game on."

∾

EPILOGUE

Cort

I stomped into the small town bar, barely registering the rustic pine walls and the scent of stale beer. A baseball game played on the widescreen over the bar, but the volume was muffled by the laughter coming from a darts game in the corner.

I didn't care about any of it. I needed a drink.

I slid onto a barstool, my weight making it creak. Orcs might not be an oddity anymore, but that didn't mean they had started designing furniture to accommodate our size.

The bartender flicked his gaze to me, grunting in acknowledgement before asking what I wanted. If I was back in LA where I lived, I would have ordered a dirty martini, but I doubted this was the bar for a great cocktail.

"Beer," I grunted. At least my drink choice wouldn't make me stick out any more than I already did. My tailored black suit didn't exactly fit in amount the flannel crowd, although it was what all the bodyguards who worked for Orc, Inc. wore. Not that I was on the job anymore.

I took a grateful slug of the beer that was placed in front of me and tried not to think about the job that had just evaporated. I'd flown all the way up to the middle of nowhere to take over from my boss, but then my protectee had run off with him and left me with nothing to do but fly home.

I swallowed the cold beer and swiped at my mouth with the back of my hand. I guess I shouldn't complain. Roc had apologized and promised to pay me for the gig even though it fell through, but that still left me stuck in a nowhere town until my flight the next day. After the year I'd had, having time on my hands was not a good thing.

Hence the bar and the beer.

At least the locals didn't seem to have a problem with an orc in their bar, but they'd had a movie shoot nearby for weeks so they'd seen more interesting things than me. We also weren't far from the mountains, so they might have seen other orcs. Orcs who didn't wear fancy suits and enjoy craft cocktails.

"You here alone?"

The soft voice didn't register right away, but when I glanced to one side there was a woman sitting on the stool next to me. I blinked at her a few times, sure she couldn't be talking to me.

Human women didn't approach me, and they certainly didn't make small talk with me. My green skin and imposing stature ensured that most women gawked or scurried away. Most men, too. It was why I was such an excellent bodyguard.

"I'm going to take that as a yes." The woman tipped her head at me and smiled, waving to the bartender and tapping the bar. "Just because you came here alone doesn't mean you have to drink alone."

I still hadn't spoken to her, but that didn't seem to matter. The pretty woman tossed her black hair off her face as the bartender slid a highball glass toward her, the ice cubes clinking.

She raised the glass high. "Cheers to not drinking alone."

I managed to lift my beer and tap it against her glass. "Cheers."

She sipped the amber liquid in her glass and ten eyed me. "You know, I don't bite."

"I think that's supposed to be my line."

She laughed, her dark eyes sparkling. "He speaks, and he's funny."

I grunted, allowing myself a small smile. I hadn't come to the bar looking for anything other than a drink, but after the last few months, maybe a no-strings hookup was exactly what I needed.

The woman drained the last of her drink and gave me a sultry smile. "How do you feel about not going home alone either?"

Suddenly, my evening was looking up.

READ the entire Dad Bod Monster series:

Dad Bod Demon by Violet Rae: https://geni.us/dadboddemon

Dad Bod Minotaur by Alana Khan: https://readerlinks.com/l/3938528

Dad Bod Dragon by Ava Ross: http://tinyurl.com/49hcfher

Dad Bod Wolf Shifter by Bella Blair: http://tinyurl.com/4cv4kmub

Dad Bod Ogre by Lynnea Lee: https://mybook.to/dadbodogre

Dad Bod Gargoyle by Fern Fraser: https://geni.us/DadBodGargoyle

Dad Bod Orc by Tana Stone: https://mybook.to/DadBodOrc

Dad Bod Vampire by Kat Baxter: https://mybook.to/Dadbod_Vamp

Dad Bod Troll by Hattie Jacks: https://books2read.com/dad-bod-troll

Dad Bod Mummy by Loni Ree: https://viewbook.at/DadBodMummy

Dad Bod Gorgon by Kat Baxter & Violet Rae: https://geni.us/dadbodgorgon

Dad Bod Minotaur Labyrinth by Alana Khan: https://geni.us/dadbodlabrynth

❧

This book has been edited and proofed, but typos are like little gremlins that like to sneak in when we're not looking. If you spot a typo, please report it to: tana@tanastone.com
Thank you!!

Also by Tana Stone

ALIEN & MONSTER ONE-SHOTS:

ROGUE (also available in AUDIO)

VIXIN: STRANDED WITH AN ALIEN

SLIPPERY WHEN YETI

CHRISTMAS WITH AN ALIEN

YOOL

DAD BOD ORC

The Barbarians of the Sand Planet Series:

BOUNTY (also available in AUDIO)

CAPTIVE (also available in AUDIO)

TORMENT (also available on AUDIO)

TRIBUTE (also available as AUDIO)

SAVAGE (also available in AUDIO)

CLAIM (also available on AUDIO)

CHERISH: A Holiday Baby Short (also available on AUDIO)

PRIZE (also available on AUDIO)

SECRET

RESCUE

GUARD

Warriors of the Drexian Academy:

LEGACY

LOYALTY

LEGEND

OBSESSION

SECRECY

REVENGE

Inferno Force of the Drexian Warriors:

IGNITE (also available on AUDIO)

SCORCH (also available on AUDIO)

BURN (also available on AUDIO)

BLAZE (also available on AUDIO)

FLAME (also available on AUDIO)

COMBUST (also available on AUDIO)

The Tribute Brides of the Drexian Warriors Series:

TAMED (also available in AUDIO)

SEIZED (also available in AUDIO)

EXPOSED (also available in AUDIO)

RANSOMED (also available in AUDIO)

FORBIDDEN (also available in AUDIO)

BOUND (also available in AUDIO)

JINGLED (A Holiday Novella) (also in AUDIO)

CRAVED (also available in AUDIO)

STOLEN (also available in AUDIO)

SCARRED (also available in AUDIO)

Raider Warlords of the Vandar Series:

POSSESSED (also available in AUDIO)

PLUNDERED (also available in AUDIO)

PILLAGED (also available in AUDIO)

PURSUED (also available in AUDIO)

PUNISHED (also available on AUDIO)

PROVOKED (also available in AUDIO)

PRODIGAL (also available in AUDIO)

PRISONER

PROTECTOR

PRINCE

THE SKY CLAN OF THE TAORI:

SUBMIT (also available in AUDIO)

STALK (also available on AUDIO)

SEDUCE (also available on AUDIO)

SUBDUE

STORM

All the TANA STONE books available as audiobooks!

INFERNO FORCE OF THE DREXIAN WARRIORS:

IGNITE on AUDIBLE

SCORCH on AUDIBLE

BURN on AUDIBLE

BLAZE on AUDIBLE

FLAME on AUDIBLE

RAIDER WARLORDS OF THE VANDAR:

POSSESSED on AUDIBLE

PLUNDERED on AUDIBLE

PILLAGED on AUDIBLE

PURSUED on AUDIBLE

PUNISHED on AUDIBLE

PROVOKED on AUDIBLE

BARBARIANS OF THE SAND PLANET

BOUNTY on AUDIBLE

CAPTIVE on AUDIBLE

TORMENT on AUDIBLE

TRIBUTE on AUDIBLE

SAVAGE on AUDIBLE

CLAIM on AUDIBLE

CHERISH on AUDIBLE

TRIBUTE BRIDES OF THE DREXIAN WARRIORS

TAMED on AUDIBLE

SEIZED on AUDIBLE

EXPOSED on AUDIBLE

RANSOMED on AUDIBLE

FORBIDDEN on AUDIBLE

BOUND on AUDIBLE

JINGLED on AUDIBLE

CRAVED on AUDIBLE

STOLEN on AUDIBLE

SCARRED on AUDIBLE

SKY CLAN OF THE TAORI

SUBMIT on AUDIBLE

STALK on AUDIBLE

SEDUCE on AUDIBLE

ABOUT THE AUTHOR

Tana Stone is a bestselling sci-fi romance author who loves sexy aliens and independent heroines. Her favorite superhero is Thor (with Aquaman a close second because, well, Jason Momoa), her favorite dessert is key lime pie (okay, fine, *all* pie), and she loves Star Wars and Star Trek equally. She still laments the loss of *Firefly*.

She has one husband, two teenagers, and two neurotic cats. She sometimes wishes she could teleport to a holographic space station like the one in her tribute brides series (or maybe vacation at the oasis with the sand planet barbarians). :-)

She loves hearing from readers! Email her any questions or comments at tana@tanastone.com.

Want to hang out with Tana in her private Facebook group? Join on all the fun at: https://www.facebook.com/groups/tanastonestributes/

Made in United States
Troutdale, OR
06/30/2024

20910146R10094